WORDS OF GRAVE IMPORT

"Twenty . . ." he gasped softly; ". . . twenty-six minutes . . ."

The sound—such as it was—stopped abruptly.

"What?" she said. "Say that again. I didn't quite catch . . ."

But this was something that the man—whoever he was—could not do. From looking very ill indeed he changed to looking infinitely worse. And instead of speaking he turned paler still, gave a great convulsive cough and fell back so clearly dead that Bridget Hallewell started back from him.

Then she saw her own hand: the one that she had put near his shirt. There was something wet and sticky on it. Blood.

She stumbled to her feet and ran and ran.

BANTAM BOOKS offers the finest in classic and modern English murder mysteries. Ask your bookseller for the books you have missed.

Agatha Christie

DEATH ON THE NILE
A HOLIDAY FOR
    MURDER
THE MOUSETRAP AND
    OTHER PLAYS
THE MYSTERIOUS
    AFFAIR AT STYLES
POIROT INVESTIGATES
POSTERN OF FATE
THE SECRET
    ADVERSARY
THE SEVEN DIALS
    MYSTERY
SLEEPING MURDER

Carter Dickson

DEATH IN FIVE BOXES

Catherine Aird

HENRIETTA WHO?
HIS BURIAL TOO
A LATE PHOENIX
A MOST CONTAGIOUS
    GAME
PARTING BREATH
PASSING STRANGE
THE RELIGIOUS BODY
SLIGHT MOURNING
SOME DIE ELOQUENT
THE STATELY HOME
    MURDER

Patricia Wentworth

MISS SILVER COMES
    TO STAY
SHE CAME BACK

Margaret Erskine

CASE WITH THREE
    HUSBANDS
HARRIET FAREWELL
THE WOMAN AT
    BELGUARDO

Margery Allingham

BLACK PLUMES
DANCERS IN
    MOURNING
TETHER'S END
TRAITOR'S PURSE

Elizabeth Daly

THE BOOK OF THE
    CRIME
EVIDENCE OF THINGS
    SEEN
THE WRONG WAY
    DOWN

Oh, what is death but parting breath?

"Macpherson's Farewell"
by *Robert Burns*

1

Salute

"The trouble with universities," pronounced Professor Tomlin, "is the undergraduates."

"Couldn't agree with you more, old chap," said his colleague Neil Carruthers cheerfully. "Pass the salt, though, would you, there's a good fellow. I can manage very well without the students, bless their tiny hearts, but not without the salt."

"You must admit," put in Bernard Watkinson, Professor of Modern History, casting an eye over the dining hall, which was thronged with young men and women, "that they do lend a certain savour to the place."

"Quieter without them, though," said Tomlin, obliging Carruthers with the salt cellar. It was a very fine salt cellar—part of a set in modern silver gilt, a legacy from a former student of Tarsus College who had made money, if not good, in the world of commerce, and who had bequeathed his collection of silver to his old College. The table along which Professor Tomlin slid it was a genuine refectory one bought by an astute Bursar of his day at a knockdown price from a monastery disestablished by King Henry the Eighth. The chairs, which led a harder life, were reproduction and were renewed at intervals by the present Bursar, John Hardiman.

A sudden burst of noisy chatter from the Buttery end of the Hall provoked Professor Tomlin into speech again.

"Much quieter without them," he said.

"That's true." Neil Carruthers always made an especial point of agreeing with people whenever he could. As he was Reader in Moral Philosophy this was not, in the nature of things, very often.

"They always do take a little time to settle down after the summer vac.," observed Roger Franklyn Hedden. He was a lecturer in sociology and always seemed to be making allowances for something or someone.

"And we always take a little time to get used to them again,"

1

grunted Professor Simon Mautby. "At least, I do." Mautby was by far the most authoritarian member of the teaching fraternity of the College, and the least popular. On his part he was widely known not to be a student lover.

"Oh, yes," said Carruthers pleasantly, "you stayed on through the vac., didn't you? I don't know how you can manage without a break, Mautby. I certainly couldn't."

"Can't leave my plants and animals," said Mautby, who held the Chair of Ecological Studies at the University of Calleshire. "They need proper care and attention all the year round. Experiments don't always finish exactly at the end of term and you can't get a good lab steward these days for love or money."

Nobody said anything to this. Everyone present knew that Professor Mautby's standards were so exacting and his views on discipline so strict that he rarely kept any of his lab staff for long.

"It's all right for the rest of you," the scientist added a trifle acidly into the little silence that had followed his pronouncement; "dead subjects are different."

The experienced Carruthers did not rise to this. Moral Philosophy, in his view, was very much alive, anyway, and likely to be kept alive by human vagary, which was not—by any stretch of the imagination—dead. Instead he remarked to Hedden, "You stayed up, too, didn't you, Roger?"

"Part of the time," said the sociologist. "I was working on my book. You know how it is—publish or perish."

Peter Pringle, College Librarian and Keeper of Books at the Greatorex Library, gave a mock wince. "I could wish there were a few more perishers about, then. I just don't know where to put books next. We've just inherited another Old Tarsusian library. . . ."

"Anyone we know?" Old Professor McLeish, Professor Emeritus of Oriental Languages, had been at the University of Calleshire longer than anyone else and therefore constituted himself the corporate memory.

"Algernon Harring."

"Harring, A.," murmured McLeish, who always thought in terms of College lists. He shook his grey head. "Before my time."

"I should say so," responded the ebullient little Librarian briskly. "He was about ninety-five when he died. He read law. Bit of an antiquarian and collector in his time but"—Pringle shook his head at the ultimate bibliographical sin—"no order,

I'm sorry to say. I don't even know what's there yet and heaven knows we'll get it all sorted out. Sixty-seven cases of books and three of letters. . . ."

"Anything interesting?" someone wanted to know.

"Law mostly. Some nineteenth-century letters. . . . I'm working on them now. They say he specialised a bit in Wordsworth but I haven't come across anything yet. . . ."

The conversation veered in still another direction.

"Is Timothy Teed not back yet?" enquired Neil Carruthers, looking round the table.

"Not due until tomorrow," Tomlin informed them generally. "He's been to Borneo or West Irian or somewhere. He did say," drawled Tomlin with deliberation, "that he was going to see a tribe out there that only fights on fine days from nine to five. . . ."

"Having us on, I expect."

"No," said Tomlin. "He says they're afraid of the dark and that the rain spoils their martial hair-dos, so they stop fighting when it starts."

"You can tell that to the Marines," said Carruthers.

"And the War Office," added Watkinson. "We might save a bit on defence."

"I should imagine," contributed Peter Pringle dryly, "that what Teed will do is to tell it to his publishers."

Professor Timothy Teed was not only Professor of Social Anthropology at the University of Calleshire but a famous face on television, and a popular writer on his subject. He was also an ultra-conservative dresser, so that when someone at the table offered odds of five to one that he changed for dinner in the jungle there were no takers at all.

"And John Smith?"

"Back."

"Ah."

John Smith was an undergraduate so daunted by his undistinguished name and so determined to make his mark that he had sought individuality the previous academic year by affecting to live by the Julian Calendar.

"Thirteen days too soon. . . ."

There was a general shaking of heads. Eccentric students, they agreed, weren't what they used to be: Smith ought to have had the courage of his convictions and come up late.

"I remember . . ." began old McLeish.

A moment later another gust of sound from the body of the

Hall interrupted conversation at the High Table. It was of laughter this time.

Professor Tomlin winced.

The only woman don present, Miss Hilda Linaker, turned her head and gazed calmly over the assembled eaters. As someone started to complain about the noise again, she reverted to their earlier topic and said, "Don't forget that a third of them are new boys this week."

"And girls," Bernard Watkinson was quick to remind her. Too quick.

She smiled faintly. "And girls, Bernard."

Professor Bernard Watkinson was one of those on the academic staff of the University of Calleshire still not truly reconciled to there being girls everywhere. He had spent a life-time in the then wholly male preserves of public school and older university college, forsaking them only for war-time service with Military Intelligence—another notably masculine stronghold. By then the monastic outlook had him in its grip.

"Better girls than enemies, Bernard," said Tomlin. "You're the one who's always seeing resident Reds under the beds."

"Sleepers," said someone adroitly. "That's what they're called if they lie low, isn't it?"

Tomlin said, "Ha, ha," in a token sort of way and Hilda Linaker went on talking.

"We've got to put the girls somewhere," she said ironically, knowing she could tease here with impunity: without over-tones. With his long, lean, ascetic face, Bernard Watkinson would have made a good monk of the strong kind, eschewing the world but not without knowing all about it—and the flesh, and the devil, too: he was no teetotaller. "And it might as well be where you can keep an eye on them."

"Girls!" he exploded as she had known he would. "We've got trouble enough without girls."

A token handful of women students at the University's two newest Colleges—Cremond and Almstone—he would have been able to understand (even historians have to move with the times), but the admission of girls to the other four more ancient foundations—Tarsus, Princes', Fairfax and Ireton Colleges—he still found hard to accept. Unfortunately for him, such is the perversity of women that his patent dislike of young ladies only made him more attractive to them. There was never any shortage of female undergraduates at his lectures. On the contrary, in fact.

"You shouldn't mind," said a very young don called Basil Willacy, well aware of this. "They sit at your feet."

They did not yet sit at Mr. Willacy's feet and he resented it.

"I'm not so sure that they listen to what I say, though," said the historian sharply.

"Ah," said Neil Carruthers, the moral philosopher, returning the salt cellar, "that's the penalty of belonging to the academic profession. Not to be listened to."

"I'm not so sure that it's not a greater penalty to be heeded," remarked Miss Hilda Linaker, picking up her knife and fork. "After all, we could all be wrong, couldn't we?"

Discussion of this novel concept lasted the High Table right through their first course.

*

The table next to the Buttery was undoubtedly the noisiest of all the tables in the Tarsus College dining hall, and the man with the shoulder-length hair sitting half-way down the table was undoubtedly the noisiest of all those dining at it. He was presently expounding loudly and at length against a rigidly structured pattern of society and a monetary system that relied on the work ethic.

"What he really means," explained his neighbour at the table kindly, "is that he had to take a job in the summer vac. to make ends meet. That right, Barry?"

"It's all very well for you, Martin. . . ." The man called Barry didn't really seem to appreciate this translation. His surname was Naismyth. "Your father's a farmer. You worked at home."

"If you think that that's any easier than working anywhere else," retorted Martin Robinson hotly, "all I can say is that you've never tried it, that's all. My father's a real slavedriver. They'd have been glad to have him when they were building the Pyramids. I daresay he'd have had them up in half the time."

"You," swept on Barry Naismyth, who was cultivating a mannered disregard for interruption (he was hoping to go into politics), "did not have to spend all your summer tarting up rusty tins for resale."

There were hoots of laughter all round at this. Naismyth never lacked a responsive audience.

"That's all I did," he insisted, "for eight whole beautiful

weeks of lovely summer. We washed all the old labels off, cleaned up all the rust with wire brushes and put new labels on."

"I was a travel courier," murmured the girl at that table. She was called Polly Mantle. "In case you didn't know, that's being a nursemaid in three different languages."

"Hospital porter," said another boy briefly. His name was Derek Doughty. "Couldn't stand the life." He paused and added thoughtfully, "Or the death. What did you do, Henry?"

"Four weeks' fruit picking," said Henry Moleyns, a dark-haired youth who hadn't spoken so far, "then four weeks on a bicycle tour. . . ."

"Of Darkest Africa?" enquired Barry Naismyth.

"Of Darkest Europe," retorted Henry Moleyns quickly, while the others laughed. Henry Moleyns did not laugh. Instead he added almost under his breath, "Very darkest Europe, actually."

"He was cycling," said Derek Doughty wittily, "while Barry here was recycling."

When the appreciation of this had died down, Polly Mantle spoke again. "I don't know about the rest of you, but by the time I'd had my own holiday I just about broke even."

"And I'm just about broke full stop," chimed in an excessively rotund student called Tommy Talbot.

This—if the ribaldry which greeted the remark was anything to go by—was not new to its hearers.

"If you didn't spend so much on food and drink," said Martin Robinson, the farmer's son, unsympathetically, "you'd have some money to spare."

"I went on the buses," said a young man with curly hair and a determined manner called Colin Ellison, who had come late to the meal. "I had no idea how hard a bus conductor worked. In future I shall always sit on the lower deck and ask tenderly after their feet."

"The present-day world of commerce and industry," boomed Derek Doughty in an accurate—if hardly flattering—imitation of Professor Tomlin's lecturing tones, "depends upon a large supply of unskilled labour, hired as cheaply as possible."

Martin Robinson rocked his chair back on its hind legs to look ostentatiously in the direction of the High Table. "It's all right, lads, Tomlin's still up there. Sitting between old McLeish and Mr. Mautby."

"Don't talk to me about Mautby," said Tommy Talbot savagely. "He just about ruined my summer."

"Came between you and your food, did he?" enquired Barry Naismyth with mock solicitude.

"You should have seen the work he gave us to do in the summer vac. All to be done before term started, and to be handed in by this coming Thursday morning first thing. Field study, he called it. Huh! We might as well have gone on an expedition."

"Now you're talking," said Barry warmly. "Iron rations are what you need, Talbot. Do you a world of good."

"It was nearly as bad," grumbled Talbot. He appealed to the others. "Wasn't it, you lot?"

"We had to take half a hectare of woodland and record the complete ecosystem—what was growing there, how old the trees were and all that. In detail," explained Martin Robinson, "and you know what Mautby is like for detail. A fine-tooth comb isn't in it. Oh, and the further afield the better, of course."

Barry Naismyth shook his head sadly. "You scientists certainly do have a hard time. Now, if you were reading economics like me . . ."

Derek Doughty grinned. "I did very well, anyway. After I stopped being a hospital porter."

"How come?"

"I've got an aunt who lives in the Shetland Islands. I went to stay with her and did my homework there."

"Bully for you," said Naismyth.

"Exactly," said Doughty. "No trees."

There was a concerted roar of approval at this.

"What did you do, Colin?" asked Robinson with genuine interest. Ellison was the leading light of his science year and strongly tipped for a First. "Study the arboreal life of an airport or something?"

"Found an absolutely ordinary patch of English wood practically at the bottom of our garden."

This provoked plenty of response.

"You would."

"It's all right for some."

"Lazy brute."

Ellison smiled. "Easy. It could have been anywhere."

"You'll get away with it, of course."

"Mautby's blue-eyed boy."

Ellison hastened to disclaim this. "No point in putting myself out, was there? Besides, I'd worn my legs out on the buses."

"Any fairies at the bottom of this garden of yours?"

"Only little ones," replied Colin Ellison swiftly, "with wings."

"I found a perfectly sweet little wood by a lake," said Polly Mantle dreamily, "on one of my weekends off, and I did my field study there. In the north of Italy."

"Ecology for ever," said Derek Doughty gallantly. "How did you get on, Henry?"

"What? Oh, all right, thanks." Henry Moleyns did not seem to have been paying attention.

"Find somewhere nice and interesting on your travels for your field study?"

"Plenty of places, thanks."

"Get far?"

"Oh, yes," he said vaguely. "What was it that came between Talbot and his study?"

"His tummy," said Martin Robinson rudely. "It stopped him bending. He only studied the trees that were bigger than he was."

"Like the *Sequoia sempervirens*," said Derek Doughty.

"Come again?" said Barry Naismyth. "It's all these long words you use. I'm not a scientist, remember. Only a humble economist."

"There's no such thing as a humble economist," began someone provocatively.

"The *Sequoia sempervirens* are the redwoods of California." Derek Doughty was going to teach and it was beginning to show. "Biggest trees in the world."

"In a minute," announced Tommy Talbot with dignity, "I shall do my Billy Bunter act and shout 'Yaroo, you rotters.'"

"Spare us that," said Barry Naismyth, deftly changing the subject without seeming to. He was going to make a good politician one day and was just beginning to realise it. "Tell us where you did your field study. I don't know about you ecologists and your trees but I can assure you that there is nothing—but nothing—that I do not know about the tin can. Its private life is an open book to me. . . . Hullo, hullo, and what does he want, do you suppose?" He broke off as a man started to come across to their table from the next one, where he had been standing talking to someone. "Well, Challoner, and what can we do for you?"

"Sit-in," said Challoner. "On Thursday. We're occupying the administration block at Almstone."

"Are we?" asked Derek Doughty blandly. "Do we have a reason?"

"Don't ask him," pleaded Barry Naismyth, "or we'll be here all night."

"They've sent Humbert down," snapped Challoner. "Did it in the vac., too. That's a dirty trick, if you like. Thought we wouldn't do anything about it, I suppose, if they did it then. We got back yesterday—"

"From Moscow?" asked Martin Robinson innocently.

"—and found he wasn't here," said Challoner, thin-lipped. "He'd been trying to get in touch with our Committee all summer."

"I'll bet he had."

"It's all very well to take that line," said Challoner, "all the while everything's going all right for you. But you'd have been glad enough to have our Direct Action Committee behind you if you got sent down."

"It wouldn't help me much," retorted Martin Robinson. "They wouldn't cut any ice with my father, I can tell you."

"Of course"—Challoner was very condescending—"if you haven't got rid of any of those petty bourgeois ideas about parental authority yet . . ."

"Oh, I've got rid of them, all right," said Robinson airily. "Years ago. It's my father who hasn't."

"Why not until Thursday?" asked Derek Doughty. "It's Tuesday today."

"Because," said Challoner unwillingly, "Humbert couldn't get here until then."

"Is he in Peking or something?"

"Ireland," said Challoner briefly.

"Seems a pity to waste the fare if he's not wanted."

"We want him," said Challoner.

"Short of a mascot, are you, then?" asked Derek Doughty.

"Couldn't you manage with something symbolic instead?" suggested Barry Naismyth. "Like a golliwog."

"Or a flag," said Doughty.

Martin Robinson shook his head solemnly. "Not a flag, old chap. It's been done before."

"No," said Henry Moleyns slowly, looking at Challoner. "You want him for something else, don't you, Challoner?"

"Well . . ."

"You want him so that someone on the university staff comes up with the bright idea of suing Humbert for trespass."

"That way," said Challoner complacently, "we get a court case."

"You need to prove damage for trespass, don't you?" asked Doughty. His father was a solicitor. "It's only a civil wrong or something."

"Child's play," said Henry Moleyns. "They'll take care to see that Humbert does the damage."

"And is seen to do it," added Martin Robinson brightly.

"Tell me, Challoner," went on Henry Moleyns, "would I be right in thinking that membership of the Students' Union is suspended when a man is sent down?"

"Automatically," said Challoner smugly. "It's in the Rules and Regulations. In cold print."

"I don't see . . ." began Barry Naismyth.

"I do," said Henry Moleyns coldly. "Quite clearly. Last time there was any damage at a sit-in they deducted the cost from the Students' Union grant, didn't they?"

"They did," said Challoner.

"And you didn't like that, so this time Humbert will do the damage," said Moleyns. "You hope that the University will still deduct the cost of the damage from the Union grant and—"

"And," finished Robinson, cottoning on quickly to this and taking up the tale, "you'll then go to law to prove that it wasn't the students who did the damage and try to get the University to court for wrongful administration of public funds or something and make them look silly into the bargain."

"Right," said Challoner. "Good idea, isn't it?"

"It's a lousy, rotten, trouble-making idea by people who should know better," said Moleyns explosively. "What they want to do is to grow up—"

"Now, look here—"

"Your lot are just playing at power politics, that's what they're doing."

"Playing, are we?" responded Challoner angrily. "Well, I'll be—"

"You just don't know what it's all about," said Moleyns with intensity.

"Don't we, indeed! I'll have you know that—"

"It's kids' stuff," said Moleyns pityingly. "Sit-ins for a trouble-maker."

Challoner straightened up, his voice pitched in a furious rasp. "I'm not standing for any snide remarks from you, Henry Moleyns."

"Humbert did nothing but ask for it all last term," snapped back Moleyns. "The man's a fool. In my opinion he deserved all he got."

"I'll have you know that five hundred people don't agree with you—"

"More like five hundred sheep," retorted Moleyns. "One dog and they go where they're told. . . ."

"I won't have you—"

"Listen to me, Challoner." Moleyns had risen to his feet to face Challoner now. He wasn't tall but he seemed to grow as he spoke. "Blind obedience to leadership is nothing to be proud of. In fact, if you ask me, it's the most dangerous thing in the whole world."

"Is Humbert bringing any friends with him from, er, Ireland?" Barry Naismyth interposed a question before the leadership and authority that was present—at the High Table—saw fit to intervene.

"He might," said Challoner, reluctantly taking his attention away from Moleyns, and rapidly regaining his normal composure. "Come and find out for yourself."

"I thought your crowd didn't believe in law and order," remarked Tommy Talbot. His plate was empty now and so he was giving Challoner his whole attention.

"We don't," said Challoner, soothed by the question, "but it comes in handy sometimes. Besides, there's no point in not using it if it's there, is there? Not if it helps the cause. . . ."

2
———————

Engagement

Not all that far away—at Berebury Police Station to be exact—Police Superintendent Leeyes was making precisely the same point to those members of the local force who were assembled in front of him.

More aggressively, though.

"Of course they don't believe in law and order unless it suits them," he said scornfully, "but then, there's nothing new about that here, is there?" He glared round at his officers. "After all, when you come to think of it, we never do have to deal with anyone who does, do we?"

This train of thought—had they heard it—would have greatly pained Challoner and his Direct Action Committee. They would certainly have challenged it. The Berebury Police officers on the other hand, owing an oath of allegiance and having a long tradition of obedience to authority, heard the Superintendent out in silence.

"And," he went on, "if they don't keep to the law, then they're villains, aren't they?"

There was someone else whom the simple extension of this line of reasoning would undoubtedly have upset. He was called Harold Tritton and he was Hereward Reader in Logic at the University of Calleshire.

"There's another thing," growled the Superintendent, who didn't know Harold Tritton and who wasn't strong on logic anyway. "The fact that they don't believe in the rule of law doesn't mean that the little—" He stopped and started again. "That the students won't expect the police to stick to it. And write to the Home Secretary if we don't. Oh, no"—he twisted his lips wryly—"they wouldn't like it at all if we didn't stick to the rules."

"Do we know what they have in mind this time?" enquired Detective Inspector C. D. Sloan. He was head of the Berebury Police Station's tiny Criminal Investigation Department and was sitting in on the conference in case of trouble later.

"A sit-in on Thursday," his colleague, Inspector Harpe, informed him gloomily. Everything about Inspector Harpe was always so gloomy that he was universally known as Happy Harry. He was in charge of Traffic Division and swore that that was enough to make any man permanently melancholy. He was at the conference because somehow everything—but everything—always managed to involve Traffic Division.

"Where?" asked Sloan.

"Almstone."

"Ah . . . Almstone . . . of course. Yes, it would be Almstone, wouldn't it?"

The University of Calleshire had always displayed a distinct penchant for naming the Colleges of which it was composed against the current trend, and Almstone, which was the family name of the Dukes of Calleshire, was no exception.

The tradition had begun in early Tudor times with the first of its ancient foundations—Tarsus College. This had been called after Theodore, the other noted Christian scholar of That Place, at a time when the stars of noted Christian scholars were definitely not in the ascendant. It had been followed somewhat ambiguously by Princes'. The Princes' were variously held at the time (by the daring) to be the poor unfortunates in the Tower (Edward and Richard) and (by the politic) to be the sons of Henry the Seventh (Arthur and Henry). The Statutes referred even more cautiously to the sons of the Monarch and left it at that.

Things had been no better nearly two hundred years later. At the Restoration—of all times—the University had chosen to call its two newest Colleges after a pair of Oliver Cromwell's Civil War generals and Fairfax and Ireton had come into being.

And when the next burst of university expansion in the sixties had come round—the nineteen sixties this time, not the sixteen sixties—the University Senate had proved just as intransigent in the matter of names. In spite of a very lively modernist lobby in favour of calling them Jung and Freud and at a time of pronounced egalitaranism, it had opted for using the family names of the two noblest families in the county. Thus the two newest Colleges were called Cremond, after the Earldom of Ornum, and Almstone, after the Dukedom of Calleshire.

"In the administration block of Almstone," amplified Inspector Harpe.

"Probably," opined Superintendent Leeyes, "the only place where anyone does any real work anyway."

"That's where their records are, I suppose," said Sloan realistically—and to avert a tirade against idle students.

"It is," said Leeyes. "All the University records, actually. In the new building there. They've considered moving them and decided against it."

"Too provocative?"

"Too heavy and too many." Leeyes jerked his head. "But at least someone senior had started to go through them for—er—

er"—he cleared his throat and searched for another phrase rather than use the word the students used—"er . . . inflammable material."

"That's something, I suppose," agreed Sloan.

"It doesn't do anything for me," complained Harpe immediately. "If half my men are keeping law and order at the University, then I can't have them keeping the traffic moving here in the town, can I?"

"It's not as simple as that," grumbled the Superintendent. "It's not actually either a criminal or civil offence to occupy a building like Almstone, remember. After all, it is University property and they are students at that University. Members within the meaning of the Act."

"I suppose, then," said Harpe fretfully, "that the clever ones are going to argue that they've got every right to be there?"

Leeyes gave a deep sigh. "They are. And don't you forget, Harpe, that they're all clever ones over there. Or think they are." He rapped his knuckles on his desk. "That's the whole trouble with the lot of them. They're all so clever that they all know where the flies go in winter and how the milk got in the coconut."

"No leave for anyone anyway on Thursday, I suppose," continued Sloan, concentrating on the practicalities.

"No leave," said Leeyes. "And," he added, glaring round at his assembled subordinates, "no trouble either, if we can help it this time. It's going to be a low-profile, kid-gloves job if I've got anything to do with it."

"What about the Riot Act?" enquired Sloan impishly. "If we're going to stick to the letter of the law and do the thing properly . . ."

"We're turning it up now," said Leeyes. "There's another thing I'm having them turn up, too."

"Sir?"

"Whether it's slander to call men pigs," said the Superintendent with dignity, "or just defamation."

*

News of Thursday's threatened sit-in had reached another quarter as well by Tuesday evening: the Head Porter's Lodge at Almstone College. The first reaction of Alfred Palfreyman, sometime Sergeant-Major in the East Calleshire Regiment, now Head Porter of Almstone, was quite unprintable.

The second was to review his forces.

"Almstone Admin. on Thursday," he mused in much the same way as he had contemplated the storming of Mallamby Ridge by the East Calleshires in 1944. "We'll have to see what can be done, won't we, sir?"

"We will indeed, Palfreyman." The Dean of Almstone—the head of the College—Dr. Herbert Wheatley, who had brought him the news, nodded agreement. He coughed and said, "There are those who wanted us to keep the administration block closed all day on Thursday to stop them getting in."

"Bad tactics," said the Head Porter immediately. "They'd only go somewhere less convenient."

"I quite agree."

"If," said Palfreyman, "we have them in the admin. block at Almstone, at least we'll know where they are."

"And," continued Dr. Wheatley, "there was also a school of thought that wanted the clerical staff to do their work that day somewhere else. Like the Library."

"A great mistake, sir, if I may say so. That would only cause more trouble."

"My sentiments exactly," said the Dean, a note of real warmth coming into his voice. In fact Alfred Palfreyman was quite often the only member of the entire staff of Almstone College with whom the Dean really saw eye to eye. Both men had their feet firmly on the ground and their relationship was one of complete understanding.

Palfreyman shook his head. "It really upsets the office people to see their files being messed about, sir."

"Naturally they don't like it," agreed Dr. Wheatley.

"Better to tell them not to come in," said the Head Porter.

"I have," said the Dean. "And we're closing the Library for the day, too."

"Now, let me see . . ." Palfreyman looked thoughtful. "We could take the locks off the doors and windows."

"We could."

"And drain the radiators."

"Water can do a lot of damage," said the Dean.

"And see that they get plenty of fresh air." He cleared his throat. "I have noticed that they don't seem very fond of fresh air."

"They aren't," said the Dean. "And it can be very chilly in October, too, can't it?"

"It turned quite cold last night," said the Head Porter. "I

think, sir, if it's all the same to you, I'll get one or two mates of mine to come along to give me a hand."

"By all means, Palfreyman," said the Dean, adding prophetically, "It's going to be a busy day for us all."

He departed well satisfied with his interview. He was not surprised to find that, as usual, he had achieved more in talking to Alfred Palfreyman for ten minutes than he did in two hours on any academic committee.

*

The Greatorex Library was in fact the obvious alternative to Almstone for a working place for the clerical staff.

It was an imposing building, even of its period, paid for out of the benefaction of one Jacob Greatorex, who had in his day successfully exploited the possibilities of that intricate system of life assurance known as the tontine. So well had Jacob Greatorex grasped the working principle of the tontine (survivor takes all) and then mastered the detail (most of the University historians drew tactful veils over this: they were not there, after all, to corrupt the young) that eventually he found himself the sole remaining member of the tontine. Being without an heir and by then much encumbered by both wealth and conscience, he had left the proceeds of the tontine to the University of Calleshire for the founding of a library.

Not surprisingly Flaxman's bust of him in the entrance hall showed a plump man, well pleased with himself and with life.

Unaware that the Dean had not only considered the idea of the clerical staff moving in, but had dismissed it too, the Students' Direct Action Committee sent one of their number to spy out that particular land. He was called Hugh Bennett. Once in the Library, Bennett made his way to one of the bays, and then went through the pretence of searching for a book and of finding it. Then he sat down with it open in front of him. He did not, however, read it. Instead he studied the Library carefully.

There was no doubt about it. Any amount of clerical work could be done here in conditions that—ironically enough—were probably a good deal better than those in the administration building. On the other hand there were no signs at all of any impending movement of the clerical force this way because of the sit-in. People were working much as usual. He caught Colin Ellison's eye from one of the Natural History bays and nodded across at him from his own position of vantage.

Hugh Bennett was still sitting in the Library when Henry Moleyns came in. Henry fought his way to the enquiry desk with some difficulty: there were stacks of books everywhere. He edged past a particularly precarious pile and said to the library assistant, "I thought they burnt all the old books at Alexandria."

"Not this lot," she responded with feeling. "Some old boy has left us all his books and his letters. Thousands of them." She peered at him. "Not that they'll interest you. You're an ecologist, aren't you? These are mostly Wordsworth and that crowd."

"Didn't he do something with daffodils?" murmured Moleyns, innocently deadpan. "That's ecology."

"That's poetry."

"I know. And ne'er the twain shall meet. Listen, my love, what I really want are books on war. . . ."

"Trojan, American, European or World?" she countered swiftly.

"World," said Moleyns.

"Bay Nine South," said the girl, adding without irony, "in the History wing. After Geography, and before Drama."

He thanked her.

"Then there's Biography and War Memoirs," she said helpfully to his departing back. "They come after that."

A few moments later a voice whispered into Hugh Bennett's ear, "Hullo, hullo. Don't often see you in here."

Bennett spun round and then relaxed. "Oh, it's you, Moleyns. I'm doing a bit of reading, that's all." He looked quickly up at the labels on the shelves in the bay where he was sitting, and saw that they were in the Modern History section. "I am reading economics, you know."

"If you're reading them from that book," pointed out Henry Moleyns mildly, "then you're a better man than I am."

"What? Why . . ."

"It's upside down."

"Oh." Bennett frowned and swivelled the book round, taking a look at the title for the first time. "That's right," he said glibly, "*Europe After 1945*. I've got an essay for Mr. Willacy. I'm looking up the Marshall Plan."

"Now you might be," said Henry Moleyns. "Not then you

weren't." It wasn't often that anyone wrong-footed Hugh Bennett and Henry quite enjoyed the experience.

"Got quite a bit on my mind," admitted Bennett in an undertone, talking not being officially permitted in the Library and Mr. Hedden being within earshot at the other end of the bay. "No real time for essays this week."

"Sit-ins don't organise themselves," agreed Moleyns *sotto voce*, adding dryly, "even if they are spontaneous."

"I hear you're not coming," said Bennett. The Direct Action Committee—to a man—were nothing if not opportunist. "What's up?"

"Changed my mind," said Moleyns briefly.

"What? Have you gone pacifist like Ellison?"

"No," said Moleyns. "It's a thought but I haven't, actually."

"You were all for us last time," persisted Bennett.

"I just don't believe in doing what your sort of committee says any more," he said, no longer whispering, "that's all."

"But last time—"

"Last time," returned Moleyns, "I didn't know any better. I was an ignorant mug ready to lap up all the nonsense your lot put out."

Bennett shrugged his shoulders. "Please yourself. It's a free country."

Moleyns gave him a curious stare. "You don't know how free, mate."

"Did I hear my name being taken?" Colin Ellison drifted across the Library to join them. "I shouldn't like it to be in vain."

"Well, it was," said Bennett shortly. "You've just got yourself an ally if pacifists have allies. Moleyns here doesn't believe that a Committee like ours deciding things is good enough—"

"Not," interrupted Moleyns bitterly, "the defence of superior orders. I couldn't stand that."

"Oh, no," said Bennett, "we don't approve of that sort of authority at all. That's what Direct Action is all about. After all, sit-ins are always anti-authority, aren't they? So," he finished persuasively, "why don't you come on Thursday? Both of you."

"Call it a waste of time, then," said Moleyns irritably and even more loudly, while Ellison gently shook his head.

"Could be." Bennett took this quite literally. "Sometimes it is and sometimes it isn't." He put *Europe After 1945* back into its place on the shelf. "The great thing is not to take anything lying down."

"Sometimes," said Moleyns, "you don't have the choice."

Bennett shrugged his shoulders. "Then it's too bad, isn't it? Be seeing you."

"You won't, you know," said Moleyns vigorously.

But Bennett had gone, his mission in the Library completed. He paused for a moment under the bust of Jacob Greatorex while he considered where to go next. Tarsus College, he decided after a moment's thought. It was high time that someone set about bending young Mr. Basil Willacy, Lecturer in Economics, to their cause.

3
_____

Beat

Miss Hilda Linaker, Professor of English Literature, was working in the opposite bay to Bennett and Moleyns and heard their exchanges quite clearly. In theory there was a strict rule of silence in the Library but she did nothing to enforce it on this occasion. It was not that she shared the views of most of the students and was against every rule *per se:* it was simply that she had long ago reached an age and stage when she was aware that some rules should be kept and some could be broken.

She, too, rarely saw eye to eye with the Hereward Reader in Logic.

The increasingly loud voices of the arguing undergraduates did not really disturb her. In fact they hardly registered on her conscious mind at all. This was because mentally she was not sitting in the Greatorex Library but in a certain cottage in Chawton, Hampshire, where an unmarried woman—Parson Austen's daughter—was scribbling away at immortal prose when nothing more trivial and conventional demanded her attention.

Hilda Linaker's monumental work on England's Jane was nearing completion now and soon—such being the way of the publishing world—it would have to go, willy-nilly, to the printers. That is, if it was going to be published as planned on the day next July when Hilda Linaker was due to retire. It was to be—already in her mind's eye she imagined she could read the reviews—a fitting end to her life's work. Then, she thought grimly to herself, she could sit back and die for all anyone would care. True, she had a Siamese cat and a sister in Surrey—both of whom would, in their different ways, miss her—but no one who would really care.

She sighed, decided in favour of positive thinking and reached for her notebook. As usual this morning she was verifying her references. She tried to do an hour of this dull but important work every morning. And as usual when she thought about her own death she thought about Cassandra Austen. If there was anyone she wanted to have a word with in the hereafter it was, oddly enough, not Jane Austen herself, but her sister, Cassandra.

"And not only about the letters," she murmured half-aloud.

"I'm sorry, Miss Linaker, did you say something?" Roger Hedden chose that moment to walk past the end of the English Literature section. "I was just coming over to tell those youngsters to be quiet, but they've gone now."

"What? Oh, I'm sorry. Was I talking aloud?" She pushed her hair back ruefully, extending the view of her healthy nut-brown tan.

"Not as aloud as those two," responded the sociologist briskly. "It's a wonder they didn't disturb you."

She sighed. "I was a long way away, Roger, that's why. Dreaming about Jane Austen, I'm afraid." She started to fold up her books. "I'm getting past it. Time to stop."

"Nonsense," protested Hedden politely. He looked over towards the issuing desk. "It's a wonder one of the staff didn't come over to stop them talking. The Library's no place for an argument."

"Oh, I don't know." Miss Linaker didn't altogether agree with that. "At least they were discussing something academic. I distinctly caught snatches about the dangers of blind obedience to authority which sounded promising."

"That's rich, I must say," remarked Hedden, grimacing. "I haven't noticed that any of them ever run any risks at all in the direction of obedience."

"Not obedience within the University," said the woman seriously. "I think they were talking about power politics."

"Believe you me," said the sociologist lightly, "they do that all the time."

"Well, then," she responded in the same spirit, "the Library is the right place." She waved a hand round at the serried ranks of bookshelves. "At least all the answers are here somewhere, aren't they?"

"Don't say that," protested the younger don. "We've neither of us published anything between hard covers yet."

"It's better to travel hopefully than to arrive," said Hilda Linaker enigmatically. She gathered up her work. "That was a good article of yours in *New Society* last week, though."

"Thank you, kind lady," said Roger Hedden. He lifted her books from her arm. "Allow me. . . ."

The woman don, who had effortlessly hefted her own haversack half-way across Switzerland on a walking tour in her summer vacation, graciously allowed him to carry her books for her.

"I take it," he said, "that we're both going in the same direction?"

"Back to Tarsus," said Hilda Linaker, "in case there's any coffee left in that pot. I can hardly believe that when I was a girl almost no one drank coffee in the middle of the morning. Dear me," she remarked presently as they approached the Combination Room via a gaze in Berebury's best bookshop window, "isn't that one of our young arguers from the Library?"

"It is," said Hedden, viewing the student standing outside the Combination Room door with disfavour.

"Did you want something or somebody?" asked Miss Linaker helpfully.

"Or have you come to say you were sorry for making such a devilish row in the Greatorex?" asked Hedden with mock severity.

"Well," said Henry Moleyns, "both, actually. I'm sorry about the talking in the Library and I did want to see someone. Professor Watkinson, please."

"I'll see if he's in for you," said Miss Linaker, going ahead.

"Or the Chaplain," added Moleyns. "He's not in his office."

"Right."

"You're not one of Professor Watkinson's history people, though, are you?" asked Hedden curiously, as the Literature don thanked him and went inside.

"No, I'm a scientist. Reading ecology. . . ."

Miss Linaker put her head out of the Combination Room

door. "Sorry, no Chaplain, and Professor Watkinson's not here, either. Try his rooms or the Porter's Lodge."

"Thank you," said Moleyns. "I will."

*

The midday meal at all the Colleges was a less formal affair than the evening one. Food was collected at a serving hatch and taken on a tray to the table of one's choice. Colin Ellison and Barry Naismyth were already sitting together when Henry Moleyns made his way across the Tarsus dining hall with his loaded tray.

Naismyth obligingly moved a stack of books off a placemat for him. "The one thing I haven't heard anyone say so far," he remarked, "is that it's good to be back."

"I'll say it, then," said Moleyns, oddly expressionless. "I can think of a lot worse places to be than here."

"You're not reading politics and economics," grumbled Naismyth. "I must have been mad to take them up."

"Agreed," said Ellison promptly. "The future of the world is with the ecologists. That right, Henry?"

"If it has a future," said Moleyns.

"Don't let's start that," said Naismyth plaintively. "Not until I've finished my toad-in-the-hole." He looked up. "Move over a bit. Here comes Mercredi Gras. He'll need two places."

"Don't be nasty," said the plump Tommy Talbot, appearing from behind them. "And who's Mercredi Gras, I'd like to know?"

"You are," said Naismyth. "Yesterday you were Mardi Gras."

"Fat Tuesday," said Ellison.

"Today's Wednesday," said Naismyth, "so . . ."

"All right, all right," said Tommy placidly. "I've got it. It isn't only politicians who are clever, you know."

"And they aren't clever all the time," said Moleyns soberly. "Politicians make mistakes, you know. Big ones, sometimes."

"Don't we all," said Tommy Talbot, who was, like a lot of really fat people, in fact very cautious. He settled at the table in between Colin Ellison and another student—a boy who was reading history and who was afflicted with a head of exceptionally fair hair.

"Politicians cover their mistakes up," said Naismyth with all the weight of his first-year studies behind him. "That's what it is."

"They call their mistakes by other names," said Ellison neatly, "that's what it is. Names like 'progress,' 'inevitable change,' 'the march of events.' Anything but the truth."

"Truth will out," quoted Naismyth with mock profundity.

"And which," asked Moleyns, "is the more important? Truth or politics? Tell me that."

"Politics," said Barry Naismyth unhesitatingly.

"Anyway, there's no such thing as truth," said Talbot, putting away toad-in-the-hole with practised celerity.

"There's scientific fact," objected Ellison. "Natural Laws and all that. That's truth."

"That's only measurement," said Barry scornfully.

"There's historical fact," ventured the historian who was sitting beside Talbot. "History's true. Like the tense in grammar. Past perfect."

"That's one thing it certainly isn't, for a start," said Moleyns vigorously.

"What has happened is true—" began Naismyth.

"You don't say. . . ."

"But what historians say happened isn't always true," said Moleyns.

"Canute and the waves?" said Naismyth mischievously.

"The death of William Rufus," offered Talbot, momentarily diverted from his toad-in-the-hole.

"James the Second's baby smuggled in in a warming pan. . . ."

The history student was unperturbed. "History's true," he said. "What the politicians say happened isn't always."

"I grant you that," said Ellison.

"But that doesn't answer my question," pointed out Moleyns.

"Nobody answers questions in a university," said someone cleverly. "They only ask them."

"Come on," demanded Moleyns. "Truth or politics . . ."

"Ne'er the twain shall meet, that's for sure," said Talbot indistinctly. He had somehow contrived a larger than average helping.

"Cynic."

"Besides, how do we know if anything's true or not?" asked Naismyth.

"It's easy to tell you're reading economics," said Ellison. "Economists can't tell the difference."

"All they're any good at is measuring the size of the fish that got away," said Moleyns.

"Talking of fish," Talbot began.

"Stop thinking about food," commanded Ellison sternly, "and think about truth versus history instead."

Tommy Talbot obediently ceased eating, and paused, knife and fork in his hands. He frowned and then said, "'And what did you do in the War, Daddy?' Will that do? That's truth versus history, isn't it?"

"That will do very nicely," said Ellison amid general laughter, while the discussion went off on another tack, as discussions in universities usually do.

*

The rest of Wednesday was devoted by both sides to preparing in their separate ways for the sit-in. Alfred Palfreyman saw to the door locks and radiators at Almstone, and devised a neat way of removing the windows from their frames. The Academic Registrar reached the end of his combing of the records in the administration office and—with a stroke of real inspiration—sent all the material he felt shouldn't be seen round to the University Archivist.

"Then no one will see it," he said to Miss Blunt, his secretary.

"Then," said that lady spiritedly, "no one will ever find it, let alone read it." A clerical perfectionist, she had a low opinion of the Archivist's filing system.

The students delivered an ultimatum, the deadline of which came and went, demanding the instant reinstatement of Malcolm Humbert. This pained not only the Dean but the Professor of English Language to whom he showed it.

"Three errors of syntax and one spelling mistake," the latter sighed. "One wonders what they teach them in schools these days."

"Guerrilla warfare instead of games," said the Dean feelingly, "and subversion instead of Religious Knowledge."

"Not English, anyway," lamented the English specialist. "I reckon we take them here these days if they can actually read without moving their lips."

The Dean read and reread the file on the dissident student Humbert before sending it round to the Vice-Chancellor. As usual, like Robert, Lord Clive, another much-tried man, the Dean stood astonished at his own moderation.

"And all we did," he remarked in tones of wonder to his wife, "was to send the man down. In my young days he'd have been horsewhipped."

"Yes, dear," said Mrs. Wheatly soothingly, more concerned these days about her husband's increasingly choleric colour than about the activities of the students.

The Vice-Chancellor read the file and drafted a statement for the press in which, though horsewhipping was not mentioned, it was implied; toned it down in the next draft; left it out altogether in the third; discarded the fourth as plaintive, the fifth as petulant and the sixth as litigious. His secretary, a realistic young woman with other things to do, did the seventh herself and got him to sign it before he went home.

"What," enquired the Vice-Chancellor's wife with genuine interest as she passed him the vegetables, "do you imagine Timothy Teed will do this time? I hear he's back."

Her husband groaned aloud.

The Vice-Chancellor's wife wasn't the only one to wonder.

Michael Challoner was wondering too.

As he hastened to point out, he hadn't attempted to recruit Professor Teed to the sit-in.

"He just told me he would be there," he said uneasily, looking round at the other members of the Students' Direct Action Committee.

"Makes for interest, I suppose," said one laconically.

"Anything for a laugh," said another.

"Will he come in plus fours, do you think?" enquired the Secretary.

"He doesn't like them called plus fours," they were informed; "it's incorrect."

"Is it?"

"Golfing knickerbocker suit," supplied the Vice-Chairman of the Students' Direct Action Committee, who was reading Social Anthropology and thus was exposed to the Professor more than most.

"And that funny jacket—Norfolk or something? Will he wear that?" asked a young man whose own garb of his mother's old musquash fur coat, his great-aunt's bandeau, tennis shoes and beads might have been thought to have distinguished him in a crowd but didn't.

"Will he wear his boots? That's what I want to know,"

drawled another young man who never wore anything on his own feet stouter than moccasins. Actually he, too, resented always being upstaged in the matter of outrageous dress by a don who dressed from a pre-war gents' outfitters' catalogue; but he couldn't bring himself to say so. "I just love his boots."

Michael Challoner hadn't been able to say: hadn't in fact wanted to contemplate Professor Teed at all. The Professor's support could well end up by being an albatross around the neck of any organiser.

"Why is he coming?" asked the Treasurer. By rights the question should have come oddly from the lips of one dedicated to the Cause, but it didn't.

"Search me," said Challoner wearily. Like many another organiser before him, he was finding his energies sapped by side issues and his own supporters more trying than a thoroughgoing opposition. "Come on. It's time we got going."

"It's to see how we behave," said the Vice-Chairman of the Committee darkly. "We'll all be in his next book, you see."

"Species *Studentius cremondii*," said the only man there to regret the passing of a university entrance qualification in Latin.

*

Wednesday evening was devoted by all the supporters of the coming sit-in to the practising of the Ho Chi Minh shuffle throughout the six Colleges of the University: and by one man to the breaking and entering of Colin Ellison's room in Tarsus College.

4

Lunge

At least, Detective Inspector C. D. Sloan was of the opinion that it was one man who had done the breaking and entering. He and Detective Constable Crosby had responded to a call from John Hardiman, the Bursar of Tarsus, made when the break-in was discovered by an indignant Ellison.

"And an amateur at that," added Sloan, looking round the disturbed room more dispassionately than Colin Ellison had been able to bring himself to do.

"But why me?" wailed that young man, much struck by the unfairness of having his room wrecked while other rooms remained just as their owners had left them.

"We don't know yet," said Sloan, while Constable Crosby set about a routine search for traces of the intruder. "He hasn't done any real damage, has he?"

"No damage?" squealed Ellison, his complexion a rapidly mounting red. "Look at the mess! Just wait until I lay my hands on the blighter who—"

"Mess, yes," agreed Sloan, unmoved. "Real damage, no."

"But why . . . ?" Ellison's curly hair went oddly with his crossness.

"We will need to know exactly what has been taken before we can tell you why," explained Sloan firmly, "and perhaps not even then."

"I'm a pacifist"—Ellison jutted his chin in the air—"but when I catch—"

"What is missing?" repeated Sloan.

"My course work, for a start," groaned Ellison, starting to prowl round the room.

"No, don't move or touch anything. Just tell me about anything that isn't here."

"My lecture notes," said the student, looking about him. He stood awkwardly where he had stopped, like a child caught in the middle of playing the game of Grandmother's Footsteps. "My vacation study—God, I meant to hand that in today—heaven only knows what old Mautby'll say if he doesn't get that in on time—it's not funny, crossing him, I can tell you—some library books—they flay you alive here if you lose library books—all my microscope slides—all my microscope slides," he repeated shakily, the enormity of his loss only just beginning to strike him.

"Money?" asked Constable Crosby with the air of one getting down to brass tacks.

This remark at least had the merit of stemming the catalogue of loss.

"I haven't got any money," said Ellison, turning to the detective constable.

"Oh," said Crosby, falling silent: perhaps even Mr. Oscar Wilde's celebrated cynic would have had difficulty in putting a price on this particular student's losses.

"My grant hasn't come through yet," explained Colin Ellison bitterly, "and, man, am I going to need it now." He waved a hand round the room. "At least this might make sense if I were a millionaire."

Sloan forbore to tell the student that—for a variety of reasons—millionaires tended to get burgled less often than non-millionaires. Instead he asked him if he had any enemies.

"The Direct Action Committee don't love me anymore."

"Ah."

"I won't go to their precious sit-in and I said so."

Sloan nodded.

"I don't believe in aggression," added Ellison rather priggishly.

"I see," said Sloan. And he did. Non-aggressors were great provokers of violence. He often wondered if they ever knew how great: especially in matrimonial causes.

"And where were you this evening when all this happened?"

"Out," said Ellison quickly.

Too quickly.

Much too quickly. Sloan took another look at the young man. It was a cool evening but he had suddenly started to sweat.

"Oh?" said Sloan unhelpfully.

"Yes, I . . ." Ellison couldn't keep still any longer, either. He started pacing up and down.

Detective Inspector Sloan, arch-interviewer, waited, deliberately allowing the tension to rise. Police in Great Britain didn't have guns but they did know how to handle tension and to use it as a weapon: to the manifest surprise of a succession of takers of hostages.

"It's like this," Ellison began again.

Sloan said nothing, professional ear fine-tuned to recognise a falsehood. He'd slay Crosby if he spoke now.

"I watched a bit of Rugby," said Ellison at last.

"And then?"

"Then I met a couple of fellows from Ireton and had a coffee with them."

Sloan's face couldn't have been more unresponsive.

"Do you want their names?" asked Ellison uneasily.

"Yes, please," said Sloan, adding smoothly, "and after you left them?"

"Then," said Ellison after another pause, "I went into Bones and Stones. . . ."

"Where?" asked Crosby involuntarily.

"Sorry." He jerked his head. "The University Institute of Anthropology and Archaeology."

"And"—Sloan resumed the initiative—"you stayed there until you came back here and found this?"

It wasn't, the policeman consoled himself, really and truly verballing. Verballing was putting words into a man's mouth—and statement. But it wasn't cricket either, what he was doing, let alone playing the game according to Judges' Rules: not leading someone on to complete what Sloan strongly suspected was a tissue of lies.

"Yes, that's right," said Ellison with such patent relief that Sloan knew that he was right: his copy of *Judges' Rules and Administrative Directions to the Police* could stay on the shelf for a little longer. Ellison said firmly, "I did stay there until they closed and then I came back here."

It could only have been thought transference that prevented Crosby from looking at his watch.

Or will-power.

Sloan's will-power.

Every man who'd ever been on the beat knew that all the University Institutes closed at half past seven. It had been nearly nine o'clock when Ellison had come back to his room and reported the damage.

"What I was getting at," continued Sloan untruthfully, "was whether anyone would know for certain that you were out and that it would be safe to break in here."

There was no mistaking Ellison's relief now. His frown cleared. "Ah, I see."

"Well, would they?"

"What—oh, I don't know. I'd have to think about that."

"Did you see anyone you knew when you were out?"

"Oh, yes. . . . A lot of people."

"Supper?"

"Skipped it."

"I see."

"Not hungry."

Sloan nodded and turned his attention back to the room itself. Children in arms knew everything about fingerprints nowadays, but they'd have to be searched for, all the same. Before very long, infants at their mother's knee would know all about germ prints, too. These days even veritable tyros at crime knew that you could tell a man's blood group from his saliva—funny that, when you came to think of it, because people had been talking about a man being the spitting image of his father since time began. Long before anyone found out about blood groups; long before they knew that father and son and mother and daughter were linked by the likenesses in tiny platelets of blood.

Or that a signpost to that blood group was contained in every deposit of spittle. Had the ancients guessed that, too, he wondered briefly, his attention caught by something small on the floor.

A dead spit, they would say, he thought, moving towards it. As alike as if the man had been spat out—not born. None of your Adam's-rib touch, he thought to himself, and then grinned. He was hypersensitive to the matter of birth just at the moment. His wife, Margaret, was going to have a baby— their first—and, just as all roads lead to Rome, so all his trains of thought ended up with the subject of birth.

He still couldn't see exactly what it was, it was so small, this thing that had caught his eye. He stooped and peered at it. It could have been a large seed of grass or an ear of corn—wheat, perhaps.

"Been helping with the harvest?" he enquired of Ellison casually.

"Not me." The student shook his head. "I'm not one of your cow-cocky ones, thank you very much. I went on the buses."

"I see. A city type, eh? Well, we'll have that in a plastic bag, Crosby, whatever it is."

"Yes, sir."

*

It was quite late by the time the two policemen had collected what information they could from Colin Ellison's room. Nobody could call it a lot.

"He was somewhere he shouldn't have been when it happened," pronounced Sloan. "That's for sure."

"And whoever did it wore gloves," contributed Crosby.

"Who doesn't?" said Sloan wearily.

"And size eight and half shoes."

"So do half this mob, I should think."

"As for the lock," went on Crosby, "it was pathetic."

Sloan wasn't surprised. The locks here were meant to keep out the casual interrupters of work and sleep: not the dedicated intruder. He stood for a moment on the deserted landing near the top of the staircase leading down to the quadrangle. In the distance he could hear noise.

"What's that?"

Detective Constable Crosby cocked an ear. "The procession, sir. I reckon it's still going on."

Sloan frowned. "What is it they're shouting now?"

"Rah, rah, rah?" suggested Crosby, who was an aficionado of the American silver screen.

"It's not that," said Sloan, listening intently for a moment to the far-off chanting.

"Could it be 'Humbert' something, sir?" asked the younger man.

"It could," said Sloan, mindful of the morrow. "Easily."

"It's 'Humbert in, Wheatley out,'" pronounced Crosby as a sudden change in the wind carried the sound more clearly towards Tarsus. "That mean anything, sir?"

Sloan sighed. "It does. Humbert is the student they want back. Dr. Wheatley is the Dean of Almstone."

"Oh," said the constable, losing interest. "Well, the people who were still in their rooms in this corridor didn't hear a thing except for the procession—nothing from Ellison's room at all. I checked."

"I shouldn't think they did with that racket going on," said Sloan absently. "It was a good moment to choose."

They started to descend the staircase.

"I wonder," mused Sloan, "what our man was really after. . . ."

"Perhaps," offered Crosby, "he just wanted to stir things up a bit."

Sloan shook his head. "I don't think so."

"He had stirred things up," observed the constable studiously. "All those papers on the floor and books everywhere."

"There was a bottle of ink on the windowsill," said the more experienced Sloan, "in full view of whoever came in. A real stirrer would have used that and then gone on to other things."

"A real thief would have taken something valuable," persisted Crosby, still smarting from Ellison's response to the mention of money. Constables weren't exactly rich, either.

"This one will have done that all right," returned Sloan briskly. "You can be sure about that, Crosby. Valuable to him.

Not to you or me. Perhaps," he went on, following a new train of thought, "not even valuable to Colin Ellison."

Crosby started to pack his notebook away. "He might have just wanted to hinder him a bit. Hold him back in class and all that."

"Ah," said the Detective Inspector pleasantly, "so that's how you got to the top of the Mixed Infants, is it, Crosby?"

"Sir?"

Sloan sighed. "Nothing. The Bursar did say Ellison was one of their bright young hopefuls." The C.I.D. man looked across at the constable, who wasn't one of theirs, and said, "I suppose, to be on the safe side, you could find out if Ellison is in the running for student of the year or the Mortimer Prize or whatever and has a deadly rival."

"Will do, sir."

Detective Inspector Sloan led the way down the dimly lit staircase and into the quadrangle. Its refectory table was not the only link that Tarsus College had with the monastic tradition. The cloister-style covered way that ran round the inside of the quadrangle provided a good way of getting from one part of the College to another with dry feet. "Now, the Bursar's office is this way, I think. . . ."

"Sir!" hissed Crosby suddenly. "Look over there—quickly. That way!"

Sloan lifted his head. "Where?"

"The other side. Across there. I could swear I saw ghosts."

Detective Inspector Sloan sighed. Far from being a young hopeful, Detective Constable Crosby was not even the brightest of the bright and it was house policy down at the Police Station to try to keep him on the less vital jobs. Then Sloan, too, caught sight of two figures dressed from head to foot in white flitting past the fluted columns of the opposite side of the quadrangle. He strained his eyes in the darkness. They were travelling at a lope that was not running but was not walking either. It was the enviable pace of healthy young men with energy still to spare.

"They are ghosts," insisted Crosby, "because I can't hear them."

The Hereward Reader in Logic would have had something to say about this line of reasoning. Even Detective Inspector Sloan, grammar school alumnus, didn't go along with it.

"Rubbish," he said briskly, adding in the best empirical

tradition (and he had learned *that* from life), "What we need is a closer look."

At first this didn't get them very far.

Constable Crosby peered through one of the bays and then reported with every evidence of melancholy satisfaction, "Ghosts, like I said, sir. They haven't got faces."

Sloan moved forward, too, the better to see towards the other colonnade. "Now, my lad, if you'd said that they hadn't got heads . . ."

The figures, which continued to progress at their steady pace across the side of the quadrangle opposite to the two policemen, were not, however, headless. As they came round the corner of the quadrangle Sloan saw them both quite clearly. He turned and said with some acerbity to his subordinate, "You couldn't hear them, Crosby, because they've got rubber-soled shoes on, you couldn't see their faces because they're wearing fencing masks, and you thought they were ghosts because they're dressed from head to foot in white. Satisfied?"

"Yes, sir," said the constable stolidly.

"When you've been in the witness box once or twice," went on Sloan more tolerantly, "against a really nasty piece of legal work, you won't jump to conclusions quite so quickly. Now then, we'll just check with the Ireton College porter on how soon our hero pops across to find two friends to give him an alibi and then we can say good-bye to the Bursar. Time we weren't here anymore. We've all got a heavy day tomorrow if this sit-in goes ahead. . . ."

*

The sit-in did go ahead.

Thursday dawned a fresh clear autumn day with a promising wind from the east. The students got to the administration block at Almstone early. They filed in and, ignoring the desks and chairs, squatted on the floor instead.

"Sitting-in means sitting down, I reckon," remarked one student to his friend, "don't you?"

"Fundamentally, yes."

"Ouch," he grumbled, "do you mind!"

"Sorry."

"It's much too early for puns like that." He hunched his

shoulders. "Move up a bit there, can you? There's a girl wants to sit next to me."

"Lucky Jim."

Not far away there was someone who wasn't being quite so lucky: the Dean of Almstone, Dr. Herbert Wheatley, who had answered the door-bell of his home to a contingent from the Students' Direct Action Committee.

No thought of anything but genuine negotiation had entered that good man's head when he agreed to interview them. Indeed, he had been hard put to it to remember to temper his natural warmth down to neutral agreement in response to this overture. It had come earlier in the day than he had dared to hope.

He received the six students who comprised the delegation with diplomatic punctilio and invited them to his study, though even as he did so the thought did cross his mind that six was rather a lot for the purpose. From that moment things had gone wrong. The delegation, far from coming to parley, had but one intention and that was to take him hostage.

"Until you let Malcolm Humbert come back," said their leader.

"Never!" spluttered the portly Dean. "And take your hands off me. . . ."

Alas, odds of six to one seldom favour the one and Dr. Wheatley's case was no exception. Besides, one overworked, overweight and highly indignant academic was no match for six fit and active young men.

"If this is your idea of a delegation," he snapped at them as they hustled him out through his own French windows and into a waiting van, "it isn't mine."

"All's fair in love and war," said one of his captors, shutting the van doors behind him.

"War!" snorted the Dean, quondam Artillery officer, still struggling. "Let me tell you, this wouldn't happen in war. The Geneva Convention—"

"That's *Boy's Own Paper* stuff now. Things have changed, Daddy-O. Didn't you know?"

They bore their captive back to the administration block at Almstone College, which was by now completely full of squatting undergraduates. The sound of chanting welled up to greet the arrival of the kidnapping party, reaching a crescendo as the Dean was hurried in.

"Humbert in, Wheatley out, Humbert in, WHEATLEY OUT
. . . OUT . . . OUT. . . ."

The noise was so great that it was a physical thing, a massive
wall of sound that could almost be felt.

"This is outrageous," the Dean managed stiffly.

Nobody took any notice at all.

The students established him in the private office of the
Head of University Administration and locked the door. As
they left, one of his tormenters, an American post-graduate
student from a world-famous School of Business Studies,
pointed to a little door.

"Dean, you've got the freedom of the executive washroom.
What more do you want?"

The Dean, positively plethoric in appearance now, began to
tell him. . . . But none of the six had stayed upon the order
of his going and he found himself talking to an empty room.

Then he realised why. The chanting outside, which had
never really died down, was starting to rise to new heights
now. It had also taken on a different emphasis.

"Humbert in, Wheatley out. HUMBERT IN, Wheatley out,
HUMBERT . . . IN . . . IN . . . IN. . . ."

The object of the exercise, concluded the Dean, Malcolm
Humbert himself, must have arrived.

It was part of Dr. Herbert Wheatley's punishment that he
had to listen to the speeches.

Dimly, in what now seemed a distant and quite disassociated
past, he remembered listening to—and, might he be forgiven,
discounting—complaints from the Administrator about how
noisy his office was: how his work was interrupted by the
circumstance that he could hear everything that was going on
in the main office. Mentally the Dean apologised to the man.
He had been quite right. Dr. Wheatley, sitting in the
Administrator's room, could now hear every word of Malcolm
Humbert's speech in the main office only too clearly.

In its own way it was a small masterpiece.

Humbert's approach was deceptively mild.

Others could make the demands, take the hostages: he
projected sweet reasonableness in every sentence. As far as he
was concerned, the Establishment had nothing of which to be
afraid. In fact, he was grateful to the authorities for showing
him the error of his ways. . . .

It was perhaps fortunate that there was no one in the room
with Dr. Wheatley to hear his comment on this.

The image presented to the seated students was one of a chastened man, Humbert referring almost shyly to a summer spent working hard to catch up with his reading.

(It had, as Dr. Wheatley well knew, been spent in the Falls Road, Belfast, where, whatever he had been doing, it wasn't reading.)

And, Humbert asked rhetorically, what was education for if it was not to teach a man to profit by his mistakes?

At this point Dr. Wheatley very nearly had a seizure.

Malcolm Humbert, student *manqué*, went on to say that he only wanted to be taken back by good old Almstone.

Cheers and cries of "Good old Almstone."

You couldn't, reckoned the Dean, still in possession of his teaching faculties, get more illogical than that.

Freedom to learn, continued Humbert in the same oblique vein, wasn't a lot to ask.

The Dean ground his teeth.

And Humbert thanked them. Whatever emerged at the end of the day—success or failure—he thanked them now. Solidarity was a great thing (cheers)—they stood . . . sorry . . . sat (laughter) . . . shoulder to shoulder . . . well, hip to hip, if they insisted (they insisted: more laughter) . . . in the cause of the right to learn.

It was perhaps just as well Malcolm Humbert stopped speaking when he did. Sphygmomanometers will measure a middle-aged blood pressure just so far and no further.

And what did emerge at the end of the day was different from what anyone supposed—and unluckier.

*

It was a girl called Bridget Hellewell who made the discovery that really lifted the day of the sit-in into the University legend league.

She was a tall, ungainly third-year student of Tarsus College, reading mathematics, with prominent cheek-bones and an uncertain manner—half unsure, half aggressive. She was really at her best only on a political platform, the light of battle in her eyes, the clarion call to victory on her lips and her strident voice an asset.

So, but for the uncertainty, might Boadicea have been leading her tribe of Iceni onwards. There, however, the resemblance ended, because Boadicea would almost certainly have taken in her stride the discovery made by Bridget Hellewell as she hurried back over to Tarsus from Almstone just after half past seven in the evening.

It was of a man clutching one of the columns of the Tarsus cloister.

As she neared him he slid down to the ground in an untidy heap.

"Are you all right?" she asked, going closer.

The man, who, even in the half-light of the covered cloister-walk, was patently not all right, shook his head mutely.

She bent down beside him, seeing his chalk-white face for the first time in the dim lighting. "What's wrong?" she asked. "Are you ill?"

The man moved bloodless lips now in response but no sound came from them save a throaty rasping. He seemed too short of breath for speech.

With some vague idea that it was the right thing to do, she put two fingers on his pulse. A rapid, thready vibration met her touch. It got more rapid even while she felt. She didn't like his breathing, either. It, too, was rapid and shallow, as if a deeper breath was painful or even plain impossible.

"What was that?" she asked, putting her head nearer and starting to loosen his shirt.

But he had only run his tongue around his lips as if thirst was a problem, too. Speech seemed quite beyond him.

"A drink?" she suggested. "Do you want a drink?"

He managed a nod at that, a nod that was no more than an inclination of his head between gasps of breathlessness.

"I'll get help," she said, making to rise. "You're ill. . . ."

Something touched her knee. She looked down and saw that it was his hand . . . a white, flaccid appendage almost beyond movement but trying to pluck at her skirt.

"You want me to stay?" she said, showing more sensitivity than her friends would have credited her with.

There was another movement of the head that might have been a nod.

And some moving of the lips that was a definite attempt at speech.

Bridget Hellewell put her head close to his mouth. "What is it?"

"Twenty . . ." he gasped softly; ". . . twenty-six minutes . . ."

The sound—such as it was—stopped abruptly.

"What?" she said. "Say that again. I didn't quite catch . . ."

But this was something that the man—whoever he was—could not do. From looking very ill indeed he changed to looking infinitely worse. And instead of speaking he turned paler still, gave a great convulsive cough and fell back so clearly dead that Bridget Hellewell started back from him.

Then she saw her own hand: the one that she had put near his shirt.

There was something wet and sticky on it.

She stared at it for a long moment in the dim light before she recognised it for what it was.

Blood.

She stumbled to her feet and ran and ran.

5

Feint

"Almstone Admin., I suppose," said Detective Inspector Sloan unenthusiastically when the call to the University came through to the Police Station. He—and most of the rest of the modest local force there—had been on stand-by duty all day long.

"No," snapped Superintendent Leeyes. "Tarsus College."

"Not the sit-in, then?" said Sloan, surprised.

"Not the sit-in," came back Leeyes smartly. "A dead man in the quadrangle."

Sloan looked up. This was quite different. "Identified?"

"Oh, yes, they know who he is all right." Leeyes pulled the message pad nearer. "No trouble there. . . ."

"That's something, I suppose," murmured Sloan, wondering exactly where the trouble was.

"His name is Moleyns," continued Leeyes. "Henry Moleyns."

"One of them?"

"He's a student, all right," grunted Leeyes. "No doubt about that. They say he's a second-year undergraduate at Tarsus

College reading ecology, whatever that might be when it's at home."

"Nature study, sir."

"Really?" Leeyes lifted his bushy eyebrows. "Well, it hasn't done him any good."

"What happened to him, then?"

The Superintendent stirred irritably. "I don't know, Sloan. That's what you'll have to find out. All I know is that some girl or other found him dying in this quadrangle that they've got at Tarsus."

"I see, sir."

"And that you'd better get over there quickly."

"Yes, sir."

"Moreover," added Leeyes, compounding his difficulties, "you can't have Sergeant Gelven because he's still over at Easterbrook on that fraud job that cropped up this morning. You'll have to make do with Crosby, I'm afraid. . . ."

*

It was Alfred Palfreyman, Head Porter of Almstone College, who took the action destined to be of the greatest immediate help to the police.

In the early part of the day he had maintained a watch on the sit-in without doing anything—just as all those years ago he had kept a close surveillance on Mallamby Ridge before the battle.

Even Mr. Basil Willacy's much-heralded and nicely calculated arrival to encourage the students with a few well-chosen words had provoked the Head Porter no further than to a quick rolling of the eyeballs and a muttered reference to overgrown schoolboys. There had been a subaltern, he remembered, in the East Calleshires just like young Mr. Willacy—about as green as they came. At least, the subaltern had been green until the storming of Mallamby Ridge. Not after. Unfortunately Mr. Willacy hadn't met a battle yet, but in Alfred Palfreyman's opinion it was exactly what he needed.

Michael Challoner, noted the Head Porter, had come and gone several times in the course of the morning, but even Alfred Palfreyman had not guessed where the students' deplorable old van had been until he saw Dr. Wheatley being bundled out at the entrance and practically frog-marched into Almstone.

Mrs. Wheatley had taken the news calmly enough. "He may even be better there, Palfreyman, than fretting here."

"Yes, madam, but his lunch—"

"I don't think," said the Dean's wife, "that missing his luncheon will do him too much harm. Or," she added thoughtfully, "his dinner."

"No, madam."

"But, Palfreyman . . ."

"Madam?"

"You'll see that they don't actually hurt him, won't you?"

"I don't think they'll do that. . . ."

And as far as the Head Porter could make out they hadn't. From time to time he had circled the building and heard nothing but speeches, and one thing that being in the Army had taught him was that speeches hurt nobody. All that he had been able to see through the empty window frames was a sea of hands and a placard which read JOIN US.

He had seen to it, though, that no one at all had gone in or out of the Almstone administration block without his knowing. And as soon as he heard about Henry Moleyns he saw to it that not only did no one enter Almstone without his knowing but physically no one left the building at all.

"Those locks, Bert," he said to his assistant, "that we took off last night . . ."

Bert opened a locker. "They're over here."

"Get 'em back on double quick, and take the keys with you."

"Lock them in, do you mean?"

"I do," said the old soldier. "Then at least we'll know where some of them are. That boy Moleyns had blood on his chest and it didn't get there on its own."

*

Detective Inspector C. D. Sloan (known as Christopher Dennis to his wife and parents, and "Seedy" to his friends and colleagues in the force) hadn't got as far as examining Henry Moleyns' chest yet. Up until now he and Detective Constable Crosby had only reached the Porter's Lodge of Tarsus College.

The harassed Bursar, John Hardiman, met the two policemen there, anxious that he had done all the right things.

"We haven't let anyone near him," he said, "and Higgins here"—he indicated the Tarsus College porter—"has a note of everyone who has been in and out this evening."

"Good."

"He closed the main gate at once."

"Excellent," said Sloan. There would, he knew, be other exits and entrances—there always were—but finding them could wait awhile.

John Hardiman cleared his throat. "The Chaplain is with, er, Moleyns now seeing that, er, everything is, er, all right."

Sloan took this euphemism at its face value and nodded.

"We haven't touched anything, of course." John Hardiman might have had a file in his hand marked "Action to Be Taken by College Bursars on the Discovery of a Dead Body." Sloan knew that the Civil Service issued one on "Bombs and Threats of Bombs."

"Good," said Sloan warmly.

He supposed that—figuratively speaking—bodies fell into the College Bursar's lap on much the same principle that the police collected a lot of their less happy jobs. If it wasn't anyone else's duty, then it was theirs. Sloan had been told that in the Civil Service, by some quirk of official irony, dealing with bombs came under the Accommodations Officer.

Since Samuel Pepys, perhaps.

Or even Guy Fawkes.

You never knew with traditions.

"And," continued the Bursar, oblivious of Sloan's train of thought, "I've sent Miss Hellewell over to Matron's room. I know you'll want to see her as soon as possible but she was very distressed."

"Naturally," said Sloan, wondering what was possibly left to come after this. Not a lot, he hoped. Crosby was getting visibly restive already.

"I have," said Hardiman predictably, "also informed the Master of Tarsus."

"Quite," said Sloan, concealing his own impatience as best he could. Death took people in different ways. It had obviously taken the Bursar by surprise because he was still trying to treat it as an administrative failure. Unless this was the way Bursars saw everything.

"The Master," continued the Bursar solemnly, "was dining with the Vice-Chancellor."

Crosby could keep silent no longer. "That lets him out nicely, then, doesn't it?" he remarked.

John Hardiman turned courteously to the detective constable. "I beg your pardon. . . ."

"If there's been any funny business," amplified Crosby with a comprehensive sweep of his arm, "then that puts the Master in the clear, doesn't it?"

This, instead of clarifying matters, clearly confused the Bursar. His frown deepened. "I don't quite follow. . . ."

"Of course," added the detective constable conscientiously, "that would only be if the Vice-Chancellor is reliable. . . ."

The Bursar swallowed preparatory to speech of a more definite kind; while Sloan charitably decided that they went too far at the Police Training School. Natural suspicion—even a simple open-mindedness about suspects—was one thing, but you didn't include Caesar's wife: not to begin with, anyway. . . .

"If," said the Detective Inspector hastily into the silence, "we might see the deceased as soon as possible. . . ."

He managed not to murmur under his breath as well, "Once more unto the breach, dear friends, once more. . . ." Bricks seemed to be dropped every time the insouciant constable was taken anywhere and the University was no exception. How Crosby got on when he was allowed out on his own nobody at the Police Station cared to think. They just tried not to let it happen too often, that was all.

John Hardiman turned back to Sloan at once and said rather abruptly, "Certainly. Follow me."

The two policemen fell in behind him, Sloan reflecting that the fundamental and time-honoured differences between Town and Gown weren't going to be anything compared with those between Gown and . . . Gown and . . . Gown and Cape . . . no, that wasn't right. . . . Gown and . . . Gown and Truncheon.

"It's not far," the Bursar was saying. "Through here and into the main quadrangle and down this side on the left and then right. He's half-way down on that side."

So he was.

Henry Moleyns was lying exactly where the girl Bridget Hellewell had left him—in an ungainly heap on the cold stone of the cloister floor, near the base of the pillar to which he had clung in his last moments. As they approached him a tall figure standing by in the shadows moved forward to greet them.

"This is Mr. Pollock, the Chaplain," said John Hardiman in suitably muted tones. "We tried to get our doctor, too, but he was out."

"They always are," said Sloan, nodding a greeting. His own

doctor hadn't better be, though, not if—when—Margaret, his wife, needed him. . . .

He brought his mind back to where he was and peered forward, suppressing an irreverent desire to quote some cynic of the past whose *memorabile dictum* had been "After death, the doctor." Instead he pulled out a really powerful torch and shone it on the body on the floor. The cold light served only to emphasise the waxen appearance of the dead face. He shifted the beam about until he had had a good look at the immediate scene.

At that moment Sloan became aware of noises off.

"I can hear music," announced Crosby upon the instant.

"The University Madrigal Club," said the Bursar.

"I think it's 'Take Time While Time Doth Last,'" said the Chaplain, cocking his head slightly, glad to be looking away. "By John Farmer. For four voices. An old favourite."

"They meet in there," said the Bursar, indicating a door half-way down the quadrangle in the direction of the sound.

"When?" enquired the Detective Inspector, wondering if many clergymen came up actually unmusical.

"Thursday evenings," said John Hardiman.

"When on Thursday evenings?" Patiently.

"Oh . . . oh, I see. . . . Quite . . . quite. . . ." The Bursar's voice trailed away. "Seven-thirty; I think I could check."

"Please do," rejoined Sloan crisply. "And would you find out if Henry Moleyns was a member of the Madrigal Club." He suppressed a stirring of pity for the dead student, who was now a member of quite a different club. . . .

The Chaplain shook his head. "He wasn't on his way there, Inspector, if that's what you mean. I can tell you where he was going. He was coming to see me."

"Oh?"

"He left me a note asking for an appointment. I said I'd see him at half past seven this evening."

"Said?"

"Well, no. Not exactly said literally, in that sense, seeing that you put it that way. Actually I put a note in his pigeonhole at the lodge."

"I see."

"So I was expecting him at my office at seven-thirty. I was waiting there for him when . . . when . . ."

"Quite so." Sloan nodded and continued to swing his torch

about. There were no obvious signs of Henry Moleyns' having been involved in a struggle with anyone and what Sloan could see of his clothing was undisturbed. He let the torchlight dwell on the dead boy's fingers. There was no visible evidence of bruising or bleeding there.

"Perhaps he was just taken ill," suggested the Chaplain, looking unhappily about him. This was a far cry from dialectics over coffee.

Crosby, torch in hand, dashed this sentiment to the dust in an instant. "Could you just look this way a moment, sir, please?" he said.

Sloan swung his torch round in a wide arc until it shone where the constable was pointing. There was a patch of something on the stone floor of the quadrangle that could only be blood.

"Not a heart attack, then," faltered the Bursar, his last chance of considering the matter routine quite gone.

"More like an attack on the heart," said Detective Inspector Sloan soberly.

*

Several hundred undergraduate members of the University of Calleshire, each of whom had vociferously applauded speakers who had declared that neither wild horses nor armed force nor even sweet reason—least of all, sweet reason—would persuade them to leave the Almstone administration block until Malcolm Humbert had been reinstated *in statu pupillari,* took a totally illogical view of Alfred Palfreyman's locking them in there.

This, it seemed, interfered with their right to leave if they wanted to, which was different.

"Is it?" said the Head Porter, deftly screwing one of the outer locks back into place.

"It is," said an Arts man with a Che Guevara moustache who happened to be nearest to the door.

"But you don't want to leave, do you?" countered Palfreyman.

"That's got nothing to do with our right to go if we wanted to."

Palfreyman, who thought that it had everything to do with it, gave the last screw a final twist. "There we are."

"It is our fundamental freedom to leave if we wish,"

continued the Che Guevara moustache, "that makes the sit-in significant."

Alfred Palfreyman, who had seen a great many fundamental freedoms come to an untimely end on Mallamby Ridge in 1944, was unimpressed. "Believe you me, young man, what it signifies don't bear thinking about and I try not to think about it."

"Establishment man," said the other without heat.

"You wanted to sit in," retorted the Head Porter, "and you did. Now we want you to sit in and you shall."

"The Committee won't like it."

"The gander never did like the goose's sauce," said Palfreyman, resorting, like many another before him, to a proverb for argument. "Besides," he added, "you aren't going to come out, no matter what, until they let your friend come back, are you?"

"Then why lock us in?" demanded the Arts man not unreasonably.

"So that no one comes along and pretends he was here all the time," said Palfreyman, locking the door and taking the key out.

"All what time?" shouted Che Guevara moustache through the door—but the Head Porter had gone.

*

Oddly enough, it was also a girl who had made the second discovery of the evening: but earlier. The police, however, did not hear about it until later.

Polly Mantle, round, cheerful and utterly self-possessed, hadn't bothered to attend the sit-in. She was feminine enough to need to belong to no faction but her own. Instead she had spent the Thursday on her next piece of work for the formidable Mr. Mautby. This had involved some study in the University Institute of Anthropology and Archaeology. She was making her way back from there to her room in Tarsus College when she overtook the Professor of English Literature, who was also starting to cross the quadrangle.

"Good evening, Miss Linaker," said Polly politely.

"Good evening"—the don peered at her in the dimness—"Polly. . . . It is Polly Mantle, isn't it?"

"It is," said the girl, falling in beside the older woman, who was stepping out with her usual vigour.

Miss Linaker hitched her gown over her shoulder. "Aren't the evenings drawing in?"

"It's quite chilly now," Polly agreed.

Their way led straight across the middle of the quadrangle, a fountain with a weeping Niobe as centrepiece being the only obstruction in their path. They had almost reached the fountain before Polly became aware of something white on its low balustrade.

"Someone's forgotten their work," she said, moving over towards it. "They've left it out here."

"We'd better take it in," said Miss Linaker. "It might rain."

"And some books," called out Polly.

"You should all be much too young to start forgetting your things like this," said the don crisply. "What will you all be like by the time you get to my age?"

"There's a box over here, too," said Polly, sounding puzzled. "No one would forget that. . . ."

"A boy?"

But Polly Mantle had gone on. "I say, Miss Linaker, come round this way. . . ."

"Maps," murmured Miss Linaker, "and . . . well, well . . . are those . . . yes, they are . . ."

"Microscope slides," said Polly flatly. "All our set have got slides like these."

"But what are they doing out here like this . . . ?"

"Colin's!" cried Polly suddenly, peering down at the strange assortment in the poor light. "They're all Colin's, I'll bet. They must be."

"Colin's?" enquired the woman mildly.

"You know, Miss Linaker. Colin Ellison's. I'm sure they're his. He had all his things stolen from his room yesterday. Someone broke in and took them, they think."

"Yes, I'd heard about that," said the Professor of English Literature thoughtfully. "How very odd."

"We must tell someone," urged Polly.

"Him?" suggested Miss Linaker astringently—but the girl had gone running ahead.

Afterwards they were neither of them able to put the exact time of their discovery any more accurately than between twenty minutes past seven and the half hour.

6

Riposte

"Well?" barked Superintendent Leeyes down the telephone line from the Police Station to Tarsus College.

"No, not well," said Detective Inspector Sloan uneasily.

"He is dead, isn't he?"

"Oh, yes, sir." Sloan confirmed that Moleyns was dead readily enough. This was not where the doubt lay.

"Not of his own hand, I hope," said Leeyes a trifle petulantly. "Too much of that sort of thing about already. Especially among the young. They take to thinking they're lemmings or something."

"No, sir, but—"

"And girls with Ophelia complexes. . . ."

One celebrated winter the Superintendent and English Literature had met head-on at an evening class. The work studied had been *Hamlet* and the lecturer had taken great pains with his subject.

So had Superintendent Leeyes.

"No, sir," said Sloan more firmly. "Not self-inflicted." That, too, was something he himself was sure about.

"Some of those students," continued Leeyes as if he hadn't spoken, "will do anything to draw attention to themselves."

"Yes, sir." As a general proposition that was something Sloan would agree with. There had been an outbreak of streaking at the University in the summer. Much-publicised. And if streaking wasn't pure exhibitionism, Detective Inspector Sloan would like to know what was.

"But not this time?" said Leeyes.

"If," responded Sloan succinctly, "Henry Moleyns stuck something sharp into his own chest he not only took whatever it was out again, but before dying also managed to hide it so carefully that we haven't been able to find it yet."

Leeyes grunted. "Like that, is it? And if he didn't do it, someone else did, I suppose."

"So, sir," said Sloan slowly, "do I."

"You'll want all the works out there, then, Sloan," said Leeyes briskly, "won't you? Photographers, the doctor . . ."

"Yes, please." The full treatment was indicated here, if anything was.

"Who have you got with you now? . . . oh, yes . . . quite. . . ."

"Just Constable Crosby," said Sloan, "and he's dividing himself between the body and some books that have turned up."

"Books?"

"Books," repeated Sloan firmly. It was, after all, a university that he was speaking from, where they had such things to excess. "Found by one of the women dons and a student called Polly Mantle just about the time the other girl found Moleyns, and not far away either."

"And pray tell me," said Leeyes at his most Churchillian, "what they were doing there at the time?"

"They are to be asked," said Sloan smoothly. "What they found were textbooks, notebooks and so forth. Believed to be the property of one Colin Ellison, another student. We're checking on that now, too."

Leeyes grunted.

"We think they were the subject of a theft from Ellison's room last night. They look very like it."

"Someone having fun?" asked Leeyes suspiciously. "They've got some pretty queer ideas of humour round there."

"I don't know," said Sloan, equally puzzled. "They were all spread out along the parapet of the fountain. Not hidden or anything. Waiting to be found, you might say."

"Anything to do with this Moleyns business?"

"Impossible to say, sir," said Sloan, "yet."

*

"'Twenty-six minutes,' Inspector," declared Bridget Hellewell positively. "That's what he said to me just before he died."

Tea and sympathy in equal proportions, administered by the Matron, a sensible woman, had had their usual calming effect and the student was very nearly coherent by the time Detective Inspector Sloan got to Matron's room. The Bursar had sensibly ensconced her in the sanatorium, bidding her to speak to no one but the police.

"And 'twenty-six minutes' was all that he said?" Sloan asked her now.

"All he had time to say," she said seriously, tears beginning to well up in her eyes again. "Then he . . . just died. Just like that," she whispered.

Sloan nodded. Death could be just like that but it was still a shock.

"I didn't realise how bad he was at first," said Miss Hellewell, still gulping a little. "Or even who he was."

"You knew him, then?"

"Oh, yes, but"—she paused in confusion—"but I didn't realise that I knew him, if you know what I mean."

"You didn't recognise him?" said Sloan, who had passed no university entrance examination in comprehension and wasn't expected to be particularly articulate.

"Exactly." She latched on to the phrase eagerly. "I just didn't recognise him, he looked so dreadful—not like himself at all—and the light isn't very good round the quad, is it?"

"No, miss, it isn't." In fact, one of the very first things the police were doing was to improve it but Sloan did not say so. Instead he went on, "Tell me what you were doing there."

"Me? I was going back to my room for some more blankets and pillows."

"Going back from where?"

"Almstone, of course. The sit-in." She peered at him, her other troubles temporarily forgotten. "Don't you know about that?"

"Oh, yes, miss. All about it."

"Well, we were beginning to get ready for the night." She waved a hand. "I'd got my own stuff there, of course. I hadn't forgotten it or anything."

Sloan nodded and got the message that she wouldn't like to be thought inefficient.

"This was extra," said Bridget Hellewell. "We, er, hadn't remembered that Malcolm Humbert wouldn't have anything like that with him for the night on account of his having come from . . . from . . . frommm . . ."

"From a distance," supplied Sloan kindly. He probably knew a good deal more about where Malcolm Humbert had come from than Bridget Hellewell did. What the police would like to know was where he proposed going when he left Berebury. Special Branch had expressed a passing interest, too.

"That's right," said the girl, "so I said I'd get some blankets and another pillow for him from my room."

"Quite," said Sloan, noting that—female emancipation not-withstanding—a woman's lot continued to be a domestic one even at a demonstration.

"It was colder in Almstone than we'd thought it would be, you see, because they'd taken the windows out and turned off the heating." This was said without rancour: sitters-in can't be choosers. "Last time, if you remember, it was summer."

"I remember," said Sloan truthfully. There was at least one man on the Berebury Force who wasn't likely to forget the last sit-in at the University of Calleshire either: the officer who was still limping.

"So I slipped out. . . ."

"When?"

"About twenty minutes past seven."

"Did you see anyone around?"

She lowered her eyes. "Only Henry Moleyns."

"Nobody else?"

She frowned. "I'm sure there were people about near the Porter's Lodge—there always are, but no one I—oh, yes, Colin Ellison. . . . I saw him and someone from the Fencing Club. . . ." Her brow cleared. "And Mr. Mautby. I knew I'd seen him today somewhere."

"Not at the sit-in?"

Her lips twitched. "That, Inspector, would be the day."

"Just one more question, miss."

"Yes?"

"Why didn't you go straight across the middle of the quadrangle? It wasn't raining or anything but you took the longer way round."

The militant public speaker, aggressive cheer-leader of a hundred rousing meetings, cast her eyes down again and said in a very small voice, "It's a bit dark round by the fountain, and there are lights in the cloister."

*

There was someone else who didn't think a lot of the lighting in the quadrangle. That someone was called Dyson and he was the official police photographer. He and his assistant, Williams, were so used to having bad lighting where they did their work that they habitually travelled with their own. Even as Sloan arrived back at the scene Williams was rigging up a powerful arc light.

"Not natural causes, then?" asked Dyson, indicating the body.

"I'm afraid not," said Sloan.

"Nasty," observed Dyson, attending to a flash bulb in his camera.

"Yes," said Sloan.

"Dangerous places, universities," drawled the cameraman.

"You can't believe everything you read in the newspapers," said Sloan.

"I can believe this," said Dyson vigorously, indicating the body, "and I certainly wouldn't let any son of mine go to one. What about you, Inspector?"

"What? Oh . . . oh, I hadn't thought." This was not strictly true. In his own mind Sloan had already decided that his as-yet-unborn son was going to have the best of everything. What he just didn't know any longer was if a university education came into the category of the best of everything: and with every passing minute spent at Tarsus College he was becoming progressively less sure.

"They've captured the Dean of Almstone," said Dyson conversationally. "Got him prisoner at their precious sit-in. Had you heard that?"

"Yes," said Sloan neatly, "but not officially."

Dyson nodded. "Like that, is it?"

"So far," said Sloan.

"They haven't told you," concluded Dyson elliptically, "and you don't want to know."

Sloan agreed. Only one thing exceeded the University's determination not to involve the police in the sit-in. That was Superintendent Leeyes's determination not to let his men go anywhere near the University unless they had to.

"This," said the Detective Inspector, indicating the recumbent body, "will make a difference."

"It always does," said the experienced photographer laconically. "Move over, Williams, I don't want your toe-caps in as well."

Williams took a hasty step back.

"Mind that spot!" adjured Sloan quickly in his turn. "There, where the chalk mark is. There's blood there."

Williams executed a delicate *petit jeté* round the patch of stone between the blood and the body while Dyson swung his camera round to the ready.

"Must have a couple of shots of the blood, eh, Inspector? The doctor'll want a picture for sure. Very keen on drops of blood, is our Dr. Dabbe. Myself, I find I like—"

"You can tell a lot from the shape of the drop," Sloan interrupted him austerely. He'd heard Dyson on his likes and dislikes before and they weren't exactly edifying.

A quick brightness illumined the covered quadrangle as Dyson photographed first the drops of blood and then the whole scene.

"I don't often do this to music," he remarked, cocking his head slightly to one side.

"Madrigals," said Sloan briefly.

"Whatever they are when they're at home," said Crosby, moving in from the shadows where he had been keeping guard.

"'This sweet and merry month of May,'" remarked Dyson, listening hard.

"We've left them at it," said Sloan. "At least we know where that lot are."

"We'll catch them when they come out," said Crosby. "The last man in may have seen something."

Sloan wasn't so sanguine.

In his experience the young were not truly observant. Not after adolescence began, anyway. Until then they saw a lot in a sharp-eyed but innocent way. Then their worlds narrowed to themselves and it was several years later before they discovered the great human outside again. After that they observed it in a way that was no longer quite so innocent but more detached.

"'When nature wantons in her prime,'" warbled Dyson alertly.

"'And birds do sing, and beasts do play,'" added Crosby in tune, entering into the spirit of the thing.

Then Williams, Dyson's assistant, turned in the direction of the sound and began quoting too. "'For the pleasures of the—'"

"That may be a chorus for male voices," Sloan said gruffly. "This isn't. Get on with it."

*

Someone else began his work by appealing against the light in the cloister, too.

That someone was Dr. Dabbe, Consultant Pathologist to the Berebury and District General Hospital, and Police Surgeon to those of the force's clientele that were already dead. He stood by the body for a minute or two giving it his whole attention. His assistant, a perennially taciturn man called Burns, had rigged up another light and was now unpacking the pathologist's bag.

"Well, well, Sloan," began Dr. Dabbe easily, "and what have we got here?"

"Henry Moleyns, student," said Sloan literally. Actually that was also about as far as he was prepared to go at the moment: that the young man was Henry Moleyns and a student.

"While what I have is one young man not long dead—within the last hour, I should say." Dr. Dabbe cocked an enquiring eye at the policeman. "Is time going to be of the essence?"

"I expect so," answered Sloan gloomily. "It usually is."

The pathologist's assistant had already—unbidden—begun to take the temperature of the atmosphere.

"Cause of death almost certainly an incised wound to the left of the sternum," said the pathologist, peering forward but not touching anything.

"Right," whispered Crosby under his breath. He was leaning forward because he was taking notes.

"Left, Constable," said Dr. Dabbe, whose hearing was excellent.

"Left," pronounced Sloan flatly. "The deceased's left." Someone, someday, was going to have to sort Constable Crosby out. . . .

"Stage left," said the pathologist, adding conversationally, "The Devil always enters stage left. Did you know that, Sloan?"

"No," said Sloan shortly. Sorting Crosby out wouldn't be easy.

"One funny thing, though." Dr. Dabbe had stooped and was examining Henry Moleyns' hands.

"Yes, Doctor?"

"No cuts or scratches anywhere on his fingers. . . ."

"We'd noticed that," said Sloan generously. As far as he knew, Constable Crosby hadn't noticed anything.

"Very unusual with a stabbing."

"Most people would put their hands up," agreed Sloan.

"I would," said Crosby immediately.

"Pure instinct, of course," said Dabbe. "Automatic reaction. It doesn't save them."

"So . . ." began Sloan.

"So he didn't see it coming?" offered Constable Crosby from the side-lines.

"Or didn't take it seriously," said Dr. Dabbe. "I expect a fair bit of horse-play goes on in a place like this."

"So . . ." repeated Sloan, thankful at least for Burns's habitual silence: back-chat à trois was quite bad enough. "So . . ."

"Or didn't recognise the weapon for what it was," said the pathologist.

"So it was not an accident, anyway," persisted Inspector Sloan. That was always something that had to be got out of the way.

"Very unlikely." Dabbe grinned enthusiastically. "Of course, Sloan, you do get some really esoteric accidents these days. There was a case the other day—"

"And not suicide?" went on Sloan firmly. That was something else that had to be got out of the way. Officially. And before the press got too excited: and before the pathologist got carried away.

"Not unless he fell on his sword," said Dr. Dabbe. "Not much of that about these days."

"Hara-kiri," said Crosby. "I've read about that. That's what the Japanese do."

"Only when they've failed at something," said Sloan dryly.

"There's no sword about that I can see," said Crosby, peering about.

"No sword immediately visible," the pathologist corrected him amiably. "I'll be able to tell you more about exactly what did it presently, but you'll have to find it, Sloan—that's your job. Unless it's still in the body, of course, and then it's mine."

*

"I don't care who wants to do what, Mr. Bennett," said Alfred Palfreyman magisterially. "There you are and there you stay."

This time the emissaries from the Almstone administration building were definitely a delegation and not a raiding party. Hugh Bennett and another man had got out of one of the windows before the Head Porter's assistant, Bert, could get all the window frames back in again. They had promptly come round to the Porter's Lodge to ask for the keys.

"Ho, no," continued Palfreyman. "We're having none of that. The only person that comes out of that building until I say so is the Dean. And the sooner he comes out, Mr. Bennett, the better, if you take my meaning."

Odds of two to one are in theory considered better than evens—but Hugh Bennett still didn't sound confident when he said, "Dr. Wheatley doesn't come out of there until he lets Malcolm Humbert come back to Almstone College."

Palfreyman, who considered himself the equivalent of two students any day of the week and therefore didn't even feel outnumbered, said, "The Dean comes out. Nobody else does."

"Not until he lets Humbert back," said Hugh Bennett immediately, though some of the conviction had gone from his voice.

But Bennett had underestimated his opponent. Neither stalemate nor an arguing match had crossed the Head Porter's mind.

"Nobody else," Palfreyman repeated, "unless you've got Mr. Ellison of Tarsus with you in there. He can come out. The police are looking for him."

7

_____

Compound Attacks

"'Twenty-six minutes'?" echoed Superintendent Leeyes down the telephone line. "Is that all he said?"

"So the girl tells me, sir." In duty bound to keep in touch with Police Headquarters, nevertheless Sloan wasn't finding the process helpful.

"And was it?"

"Was it what, sir?"

"Twenty-six minutes past seven," snapped Leeyes, whose approach to most things was literal. "Didn't you ask the girl?"

"She thought she found him just before the half hour, sir."

"So the time matters," concluded Leeyes speedily, "doesn't it?"

"I don't know, sir," said Sloan. "Not yet."

"Come, come, Sloan," said the Superintendent testily, "men don't waste their dying breaths on saying things that don't matter, do they?"

Sloan himself drew breath. King Charles the Second's "Let not poor Nelly starve" was the first quotation that came into his mind. Sergeant Gelven, at least, would have said that that was important. He was the fattest man on the station.

"Do they?" repeated Leeyes.

Sloan searched his mind. There had been something he'd learnt at school . . . what was it now . . . and then it came to him: "Crito, we owe a cock to Aesculapius."

"What?" enquired Leeyes.

He must have said it aloud.

"Socrates," said Detective Inspector Sloan uncertainly, "I think." A grubby schoolboy when he'd first heard that, he'd never thought that he would ever call it to mind again. "Last words."

"Well, they're important, aren't they?" said Leeyes largely. "Out of debt, out of danger."

Sloan hadn't thought of that aspect of the ancient philosopher's remark.

"He wouldn't have wanted to die owing," said the Superintendent. "Not him."

"No, sir," agreed Sloan hastily, blessing some long-forgotten schoolmaster. Perhaps now—who knows—he would find a use for Pythagoras' Theorem. The Geometry teacher had always insisted that everyone ought to be able to prove Pythagoras. Sloan could—or rather, had once—but hadn't found the fact helpful in life so far.

"Twenty-six minutes," mused the Superintendent. "Funny time."

"We think he was on his way to an appointment with the Chaplain," offered Sloan, "at seven-thirty."

"Was he now?" said Leeyes quickly. "What for?"

"We don't know. He made an appointment with the Chaplain without saying what it was about."

"We can't read too much into it, then, can we?" said the Superintendent.

That, thought Sloan to himself, was rather good coming from a man who had decided that William Shakespeare was an atheist solely on the strength of Hamlet's final "The rest is silence."

"It might matter, sir," said the Detective Inspector. "Too soon to say."

"Anything else come to light?"

"Henry Moleyns wouldn't go to the sit-in," said Sloan slowly. "Apparently he had quite an argument about it in Hall on Tuesday evening with a man called Challoner."

"He's one of the trouble-makers, isn't he?" The Superintendent had the true policeman's memory for the bad lot.

"Number two after Humbert, I should say."

"Find out about that, then, Sloan."

"Yes, sir."

"Anything else?"

"Dr. Dabbe says that the weapon—"

"Tut, tut," said Leeyes reprovingly, "don't you know that 'weapon' is an emotive word?"

"Yes, sir." And he knew all about the emotions the use of weapons aroused, too, but he did not say so.

"Can't have you using that," said Leeyes. "As good as a red rag to some of our lady magistrates."

"No, sir," said Sloan impassively. "Of course not."

"Weapon implies attack . . ." The Superintendent's voice became an elephantine parody of someone in Court.

"He was attacked," Sloan began again.

"I know he was. You know he was. He knows he was." Leeyes came to the end of his declension and said smartly, "But that doesn't mean that we'll be able to get away with saying so in court just like that."

Unmoved, Sloan started yet again. "Dr. Dabbe has described the nature of the instrument which caused the penetrating wound, sir."

What you thought and what you said in court were horses of such different colours—and as far as the police were concerned always would be—that Sloan saw no irony where none was intended.

"That's better," said Leeyes. "Now, what about this instrument?"

"Sharp, sir."

"That all?"

"So far. The doctor's going to do a post mortem straight away."

"Good."

"I shall want some help, sir, please. A woman police officer, for the night."

"Right."

"That all?"

"Yes, sir."

Leeyes grunted. "What about the Dean of Almstone?"

"Still prisoner."

*

"Poor Wheatley," said Kenneth Lorimer. "He won't be very happy, will he?"

The Dean of Almstone, Dr. Herbert Wheatley, might still have been safely in baulk in his own administrative block, but the Master of Tarsus, Professor Kenneth Lorimer, was still very much in play. This might have been due to chance. He had been in London all day doing battle at a University Grants Committee meeting and had thus not been available for kidnapping.

The expression "Dining with the Vice-Chancellor" which had been so readily bandied about by John Hardiman, the Bursar, earlier in the evening, had been merely a cover story for a prolonged conference of such heads of the six Colleges as were still at liberty. They were gathered in his sitting-room.

"Well, gentlemen," said the Vice-Chancellor as the coffee cups circulated, "are we agreed to continue our policy of masterly inactivity?"

The others gravely acknowledged the pun and nodded their assent. The various alternatives to doing nothing had in any case all been thoroughly canvassed over the past hour: and been dismissed in turn as mostly wishful thinking.

"Palfreyman tells me," went on the Vice-Chancellor, "that they haven't injured Wheatley or anything."

"I'm glad to hear it," said the Dean of Ireton briskly. The term before, he himself had been severely bruised about the left eye while attempting to introduce a distinguished but unpopular speaker who had come to address a meeting at Ireton College. The distinguished speaker had not only never had a hearing ("Democracy in Danger" had been his subject) but had been covered in flour for his pains.

"And Wheatley hasn't made any concessions, I hope," said Lorimer of Tarsus hawkishly. Professor Lorimer had made none at all at the University Grants Committee meeting and was still feeling militant.

"None," declared the Vice-Chancellor. "Malcolm Humbert doesn't come back."

"Can't we get rid of Challoner too?"

"Not legally," answered the Vice-Chancellor with precision.

"Timothy Teed's in there with them, I take it?" said the Dean of Ireton. "Making the most of it all for his next programme. . . ."

"He is."

"What's he wearing?"

"A deer-stalker."

"He would."

"The cameras will pick that out all right."

"Bound to."

"He never misses a trick, does he?"

It was at this point that the news of the stabbing of a student reached them; and the Vice-Chancellor made a remark also destined to go down in the annals of the University of Calleshire:

"Really," he said, "this is going too far."

*

"They haven't stopped singing, sir," announced Detective Constable Crosby as Sloan got back to the quadrangle after telephoning the Superintendent.

"Good. At least we know where they've been all evening."

"'A pretty bonny lass was walking,'" chorused the University Madrigal and Glee Club. "'In the midst of May before the sun 'gan rise.'"

"No one's come out," went on Crosby, "and everything else is quiet."

"Good," said Sloan again, casting his eye along the paved way. All that now remained of the earlier drama was some chalk lines on the stones. The late Henry Moleyns had been cocooned in polythene and removed to Dr. Dabbe's mortuary while—the thickness of a wall away from sudden death—the singing had gone on.

"I don't know how they keep it up, I'm sure," said Crosby as the next two lines of the madrigal drifted over the quiet quadrangle.

"Let's find out," suggested Sloan.

"Listen to them, sir."

"'I took her by the hand and fell to talking,'" sang the undergraduates, "'Of this and that, as best I could devise.'"

"They've had half a dozen goes at this one already," said the constable as the final strains of the madrigal came over the still evening air. "I know it by heart now."

"'Heart' seems to be the operative word with madrigals," observed Sloan, moving towards the door leading to the singers.

"'I swore I would, yet still she said I should not,'" trilled the madrigalists. "'Do what I would, and yet for all I could not.'"

"They get into a muddle with that part sometimes," said Crosby.

"I'm not surprised," said Sloan vigorously, "but all the same I still think I prefer it to 'Humbert in, Wheatley out.' Come on. . . ."

Inside the Madrigal and Glee Club meeting were not only singers but musicians. A large girl in a voluminous smock was strumming a strange instrument as they entered, while a weedy youth was blowing away at one nearly as tall as himself. Four singers were standing in the middle of the room, their mouths wide open, for all the world, thought Sloan, like four little birds in a nest waiting for worms.

"There's some funny folk about even without looking in the mirror," muttered Crosby into Sloan's right ear.

"Police," said Sloan loudly.

This group of undergraduates was not of the stuff of which militant demonstrators are made.

"Were you looking for someone?" asked their leader politely.

"The last man in here tonight," said Sloan.

"Stephen," they said with one accord, pointing.

"Me," said a bespectacled boy with tow-coloured hair, who was sitting among the musicians with a very tiny instrument in his hand. It bore a close resemblance to the tambourine which Sloan remembered from his own first year at infant school and to the best of his recollection had not seen since.

"Stephen?"

"Stephen Smithers," he said, laying down his instrument. "I was last, I know, because I was late."

"At least three minutes," said the leader.

"Nearer five," said the large girl in the smock censoriously. It was a decidedly unbecoming garment on one so large. "We couldn't start with an air."

"More like ten minutes," said someone else.

"Which wouldn't have suited the Duke of Wellington," said one of the singers.

Sloan turned enquiringly towards the last speaker.

"Great on punctuality was the Duke," the young man said, adding by way of explanation, "I'm reading History."

"Ah," said Sloan. "And what would the rest of you be doing?"

Of the eight it emerged that two were reading English, only one Music, one was going to be a linguist (the fat girl), two were reading Theology (more musical clergymen, thought Sloan) and one was reading Politics.

"Politics?" echoed Sloan. "What's your name?"

"Barry Naismyth."

Sloan was quite relieved that the voice was deep. Sexing students these days could be as highly skilled as sexing chickens except that you didn't get paid for it. Naismyth's hair was as long as any girl's and—which was worse—curly, and his clothes totally and quite deliberately epicene.

"And if you want to know why he isn't at the sit-in," began the historian smugly.

"Yes?" said Sloan, intrigued.

"It's because he's just read the life history of Napoleon Bonaparte."

Naismyth started to protest.

"Has he?" said Sloan. He considered the historian. "And you're going to tell me what that's got to do with his missing the sit-in, aren't you?"

The speaker grinned. "Yes, I am."

"It's got nothing to do with it," interposed Barry Naismyth hastily. "Nothing at all."

"Just as Napoleon was first beginning in politics after he left Corsica something a bit troublesome cropped up—"

"The French Revolution," said Sloan. There had been a lecturer at the Police College who dated all disorder from that: Cromwell's English Republic had been an orderly one.

"Yes, well"—the student was clearly surprised—"when Napoleon could see that everyone was going to get egg on their faces, what did he do?"

"You tell me," suggested Sloan, "then I'll know, won't I?"

"Galloped off in the opposite direction, that's what. Went off on a long campaign somewhere else. Italy, I think."

"I'll let you into a little secret," said Sloan. "It's been done before."

"Not news?" said the history student sadly.

"Not news," said Sloan. "A lot of politicians duck when they see trouble coming. They get diplomatic illnesses." His manner sobered suddenly. "And then they leave the dirty work to the police." He looked round the room. "And the rest of you? Why weren't you at the sit-in? Have you all got Napoleon complexes or what?"

"It was our Club night," said the girl in the smock earnestly. "That's why we didn't go."

"We're rehearsing for a concert, too," said one of the incipient clergymen.

"If wet, in village hall," muttered Crosby.

Sloan pulled himself together. "Now, then, Mr. Smithers, can you spare us a moment. . . ."

The chief impediment to interviewing Stephen Smithers was his sneeze.

"Sorry," he sniffed. "Hay-fever."

"You were late at the meeting," observed Sloan.

"Had to get some more tissues," he explained. "Run out. I buy them by the hundred now. Ah . . . ah . . . ah . . . atishoo!"

"Sneeze on Monday, sneeze for danger," said Detective Constable Crosby.

"When should you have been there?" asked Sloan valiantly, where a lesser man would have turned upon his assistant.

"Seven-thirty but . . . atishoo . . . sorry . . . I wasn't."

"So we hear."

"They had to start with a madrigal," said Smithers. "No glee without me."

"No glee." Crosby wrote that down. Sloan wondered what the Superintendent would make of it.

Smithers sneezed again.

"Sneeze on Tuesday, sneeze for sorrow," said Crosby.

"How late were you?" asked Sloan rather sharply.

"They'd got to the end of John Wilbye's 'Cloris,'" said Smithers helpfully, "so I expect we can work it out if it's important." He looked alertly from one policeman to the other. "It is important, isn't it?"

"Oh, yes," said Sloan, "it is important."

"Couldn't stop sneezing, you see." He was fumbling for a

tissue even as he spoke. "It's even worse first thing in the morning. They say," he managed between sneezes, "that all this hay-fever's come from a new strain of Canadian wheat that they've brought into England these last few years but I don't know, I'm sure. All I know is—"

"This evening," said Sloan implacably.

"Yes?"

"Did you see anyone as you came along?"

"Plenty of people. Had you anyone in mind, Inspector?"

"Henry Moleyns."

Smithers shook his head. "Not him. At least, not that I remember."

"Did you see anyone at all you knew?"

Smithers screwed his face up as for another sneeze but this time it signified the effort of recollection. "Colin Ellison—I saw him on the stairs. Someone from the Fencing Club and Miss Linaker. She was in a hurry like me. There were people about, you know. There always are."

"Did you cross the quad or go round?"

"Across," said Smithers promptly. "Saves time. I knew I was late."

"Did you see anything unusual by the fountain?"

"Nothing," sneezed Smithers. "Should I have done?"

"Not," said Sloan precisely, "if there wasn't anything there unusual to see at the time."

*

Over in the Combination Room at Tarsus College old, old Professor McLeish was taking a detached—not to say totally academic—view of the news of the death of Henry Moleyns.

"I think," he said, "that the last time that we had an undergraduate of this University actually killed on the premises, so to say, was in 1797—or was it 1798—yes, perhaps it was in 1798. . . ."

One of the young scientists present who still believed in accuracy above all for its own sake (and even more naïvely believed that other people felt the same) waited on principle for him to decide.

Nobody else did.

"What happened then?" enquired Professor Tomlin curiously.

"A duel."

"Ah." Professor Tomlin gave a wolfish smile. "Pistols for two, breakfast for one."

"If my memory serves me correctly," said old McLeish complacently, "it was over a lady." In fact his memory was excellent and few people knew enough to contradict him anyway.

"Boys will be boys," muttered Roger Hedden *sotto voce*.

"Or it might have been a matter of honour between gentlemen," said the old man.

Those in the Combination Room treated this as the un-likeliest explanation of all.

"That's out these days," said someone quickly.

"And how!" added the College's classicist, who was for some reason curiously addicted to modern slang—taking his revenge on the live tongue for the invulnerability of the dead ones, his colleagues thought. "There isn't much of that about these days."

"And as for the lady's honour . . ." began Bernard Watkinson, the misogynist.

"Nobody seems to think that's worth fighting for anymore either," agreed Tomlin mournfully. He was much-married to the daughter of a Bishop who found it impossible to keep abreast of changing standards and lamented the fact *ad nauseam*.

"I believe that there was some suggestion," rumbled on old McLeish, "that our Jacob Greatorex had—er—an insurable interest in the outcome of the duel."

"Very probably."

"I shouldn't think anyone is going to gain from young Moleyns' dying," said someone. "He's an orphan. Brought up by a maiden aunt, I believe."

"Poor Moleyns," said Hedden ambiguously. "I wonder what really happened?"

This, as is usually the way with the first instalment of bad news, nobody seemed to know. And—as again is the way with bad news—they were about to go over the same ground all over again when they were joined by an irate Professor Simon Mautby. He erupted into the Combination Room in a fine state of outrage.

"Just wait," he stormed. "Just wait until I get my hands on them. That's all. Just wait—then I'll—I'll—"

"Hands on whom?" enquired Tomlin.

"Whoever's been in my lab without my permission," snapped Mautby. "That's who. And when I do I'll—"

"And what did they do in there?" asked Tomlin with the maddening calm that men reserve for other people's difficulties.

"Do!" exploded Mautby. "They opened one of the animal cages there, that's what they did. And when I catch them I'll—"

It wasn't that words showed any sign of failing the Professor of Ecology. It was just that he was interrupted before he could get on to the fine detailing of the hanging, drawing and quartering that was obviously in store for whoever had illicitly entered his precious laboratory.

"What happened as a consequence of this cage being opened?" enquired the junior scientist earnestly. After all, *Penicillium* had been discovered by much the same sort of accident.

"Some white mice got out," said Mautby tightly.

Nobody in the Combination Room so much as tittered.

"And?" enquired Watkinson gravely.

"And one of them used one of my heated propagating trays for the accouchement of her family. . . ."

8
_____

Prises de Fer

Detective Constable Crosby's initial examination and subsequent sealing up of Henry Moleyns' room in Tarsus College was following the orthodox pattern he had been taught at his Police Training College. As far as he was concerned he was not looking for anything in particular and, if asked, would have replied that he was carrying out a routine procedure.

He did, however, find something.

But not immediately.

The room was a pigeon pair with that occupied by Colin Ellison, which he had seen the evening before—and no doubt with a hundred others, too. Crosby's search of it was not done on "Hunt the Thimble" lines. It was, on the contrary, done very methodically indeed. Constable Crosby would have found Edgar Allan Poe's purloined letter first time round.

He began with the bed. He had once found a shot-gun under a mattress—only just before its owner reached it, too—and now he always looked there first. There was nothing under Henry Moleyns' mattress, nor, as it happened, under the bed either. The College beds were high, narrow and well-castored for ease of making. In spite of all these things Henry Moleyns' bed had been no more than cursorily pulled together to give the semblance of tidiness. A complete search of it yielded nothing whatsoever.

Crosby then turned his attention to the built-in cupboard that served the office of a wardrobe. It was behind the hanging dresses here that ladies usually kept that which they did not want found.

Bottles, as a rule.

All that Henry Moleyns had hanging up in his wardrobe were a couple of jackets and some two or three pairs of trousers. Behind the door was a style of windcheater called a combat jacket by young men who had never known the meaning of the word. The University authorities in their wisdom did not provide dressing tables for their Malvolios. Instead there was a tallboy with a mirror beside it on the wall.

Crosby went through the drawers of this one by one. He performed the operation police-fashion by taking them out in turn, placing each one on the bed and examining both the contents and the drawer itself. The pinning of stolen property to the outside back of a drawer had been known to happen in criminal circles. It had not happened here. In fact the drawers contained nothing more than a student might have been reasonably expected to need in the way of clothes for the autumn term.

Beside the tallboy was a shoe-rack. Crosby stopped to look at Moleyns' shoes. Shoes told you such a lot about a man—how he walked, rich or poor, particular or careless and, as often as not, where he'd been. Poor but particular, decided Crosby a moment later. And the student had walked quite firmly on the centre of the sole without scuffing heel or toe. As to where he'd been, there was nothing to show that without using a microscope. Deciding to leave any hunting of the slipper to others, he turned his attention to Moleyns' desk.

Here again there was a marked likeness to Colin Ellison's

possessions. Crosby mentally ticked off a list of items that it seemed no ecology student should be without—lecture note-books, textbooks, microscope slides, course work . . . as far as he could tell, in Henry Moleyns' case they were all present and correct, but other and more expert eyes would also have to check on that.

The desk itself was not of the tidiest. Lecture schedules jostled with Club notices—Moleyns would seem to have been a member of the University Fencing Club and the Tarsus Debating Society—while the University Calendar itself and the Collegiate Church Kalendar (in this setting Constable Crosby unhesitatingly laid the disparity in spelling at the printer's door) took pride of place on the much-pinned wall behind the desk. Of a more personal nature there was very little, and nothing of moment on the desk itself. Then he pulled open the first of the three drawers—and became very thoughtful indeed. . . .

Later he moved over to the bookcase, which was also a standard fitment. There were more textbooks here, and plenty of paperbacks—which, though they could be said to be loosely about the study of nature, were also about a decidedly extra-curricular aspect of it. Whoever told them that Henry Moleyns hadn't got a steady girl friend might well have been right. It did not mean that his mind was elsewhere.

The wastepaper basket yielded a short, screwed-up note from the Reverend C. A. T. Pollock, University Chaplain, saying that he would be happy to see Henry Moleyns in his office at 7:30 P.M. on Thursday evening as requested. Crosby retrieved this and laid it carefully on one side.

He then returned to the centre of the room and stood there as he had done when he first came in, trying to recapture a feeling that he had had when he had entered the room earlier.

He did his best to explain this to Inspector Sloan afterwards. "A funny feeling, sir."

"Yes?" Funny feelings were not encouraged at Berebury Police Station.

"I didn't know what it was at first."

"And what was it?" enquired Sloan with what patience he could muster. It had been a long day and it wasn't over by any means.

"That someone else had been and done a search ahead of me."

Sloan looked up alertly. "What makes you say that?"

"This feeling, sir. . . ."

"And what else?"

"The top drawer of the desk."

"What about it?"

"Everything in it was the wrong way round."

"Upside down?"

"Back to front."

"Ah. . . ." Sloan let out a sigh. The boy was learning something after all.

"You wouldn't sit at a desk and put everything in it facing the wrong way, would you, sir?"

"No," agreed Sloan thoughtfully, "you wouldn't."

"Bit if you'd emptied the drawer quickly, looking for something . . ."

"And found it," said Sloan pessimistically. It was obviously going to be this sort of a case.

"And then been disturbed and had to put everything back quickly . . ."

"You'd have been standing, of course," said Sloan, tacitly accepting the argument, "working from above."

"In a hurry, too, sir."

"So if you heard someone coming you'd just stuff everything back from where you stood."

"Yes, sir."

Sloan looked up. "What wasn't there?"

"I don't know, sir," said Crosby, not unreasonably.

"We shall need to know."

"Yes, sir."

"Well done, anyway," said Sloan absently. "Find anything else?"

Crosby coughed. "Yes, sir, there was something else."

"Tell me," commanded Sloan.

The detective constable produced a small plastic bag, duly sealed and labelled. Lying in the bottom of it was a solitary seed of wheat. "I just happened to notice it, sir," he said modestly.

"Where?" barked Sloan impatiently.

"In the bottom of his wardrobe."

"Trouser turn-ups, I'll be bound," breathed Sloan, beaming. "The greatest gift to forensic science after fingernails. . . . Here, pass me that telephone."

*

"What the devil," demanded Superintendent Leeyes a moment or so later, "was Henry Moleyns doing stealing stuff from Ellison's room?"

"We don't know yet if both ears of wheat are the same, sir," Sloan said cautiously. "They only look alike to me."

The Superintendent dismissed this as mere quibbling.

"Moreover," continued Sloan energetically, "we don't know if Henry Moleyns was the one who had stolen Ellison's things. After all, someone else might have got into both rooms."

"And crouched at the back of the wardrobe?" enquired Leeyes acidly. "Be your age, Sloan."

"Yes, sir." Sloan sighed. He certainly felt it today. He'd need more vigour than this if he was going to show his son how to keep his cricket bat straight in ten years' time.

"That wheat came from Henry Moleyns' clothes all right," decided the Superintendent. "You'd better do another search of his rooms."

"Yes, sir."

"And his home, wherever that may be."

"It was in Luston, sir." A shocked aunt was even now on her way over to Berebury from there to see Sloan. Someone was going to have to show her Henry Moleyns' body. It sounded such a simple procedure as ordained in *Jervis on Coroners. . . .*

"And this man who had his things stolen yesterday. . . ."

"Colin Ellison," said Sloan, "and 'removed' might be a better word than 'stolen,' seeing as we think they've all turned up."

"Don't come the Theft Act with me, Sloan," rumbled Leeyes, changing tack suddenly. "It's given me quite enough trouble as it is."

"Sorry, sir."

"It was meant to stop argument and all it's done is cause it."

"Yes, but these things of Ellison's on the fountain parapet—"

"It's always the same with new legislation," went on Leeyes, undiverted. The mere sighting of a hobby-horse was enough to set him off.

"Yes, sir," agreed Sloan—and meant it. It was only since he had been a working policeman that he had realised why it was that they had given King Alfred the extra title of "Great." To be a good lawgiver you had to be really great.

"They always think they're improving things, Sloan."

"Motives of the highest, sir," said Sloan. It didn't do to argue with Superintendent Leeyes, and in any case the Superintendent's thinking on criminality hadn't really advanced since certain tablets had come down from Mount Sinai and it wasn't likely to make any progress now.

"This Colin Ellison, then," said Leeyes grandly, "you'd better give his room another going-over too."

"Yes, sir."

"And find out where he comes into things."

"That's not really clear yet," said Sloan frankly.

"Where is he?"

"We're not too sure about that, either," admitted Sloan. "We are looking for him. . . ."

"Ah . . ."

"But we haven't found him so far. He's not at the sit-in."

"Last seen?"

"In the quadrangle," said Sloan.

"When?"

"About seven-thirty," said Sloan unhappily.

"Ah," said Leeyes—just as Sloan had known he would.

"You don't," ventured the Detective Inspector, "usually stab people in the chest for stealing your notebooks."

"Sloan," said Leeyes irately, "I won't have you coming that 'it can't be him because it's too easy' line with me."

"I'm not, sir."

"Because," said the Superintendent, totally unheeding, "if the villain wasn't nearly always the most obvious person in sight this new generation of constables would never even know which collar to feel."

"No, sir."

"If Ellison's gone to earth—and if that's not a guilty action I don't know what is—you'd better find him quickly."

"Yes, sir." Sloan coughed. "There was something else, sir."

He told the Superintendent about Crosby's theory that someone else had searched Moleyns' rooms before him.

"And not for stray ears of wheat either, I take it?" concluded Leeyes.

"No, sir. The desk." He explained about the papers in the drawer.

"And Crosby's quite sure it wasn't just Moleyns putting the contents back wrongly himself?"

"He took the trouble to do it with gloves on if he did," said Sloan succinctly. There was one thing that could be said about Crosby. There was no one to touch him with a can of

Aluminium No. 1 Finger-print Powder. "And all we know about whoever it was is that they had the regulation number of fingers and thumbs."

"Anything else there?" enquired Leeyes.

"Just the note from the Chaplain. We knew Moleyns had made an appointment to see him because Mr. Pollock told us."

"What about?"

"That we don't know," said Sloan, "and neither does the Chaplain. It could have been about almost anything, I suppose. . . ."

"Saw one once myself," said Leeyes unexpectedly.

"Sir?"

"Before we went ashore at Walcheren in '44. The Brigadier seemed to think we should." He grunted. "In case we had anything to declare to St. Peter, I suppose. You know what soldiers are."

"Yes, sir." And he did, too.

"Told him I was a copper," said Leeyes reflectively, "and that shut him up."

"It does most people," said Sloan. It went with the job, did that. It wasn't only the hours that were unsocial. Even if you said you were a copper's wife most people fell silent—or so his own wife, Margaret, told him. He wondered how a copper's wife's son would get on. . . .

Leeyes was still talking: ". . . and then I said that I believed in law and order and the enemy didn't and as far as I was concerned that was that."

Sloan felt a pang of sympathy for some anonymous cleric. A faith as simple as the Superintendent's must have been refreshing but hardly textbook.

"He was an Army Chaplain, of course, Sloan."

"Naturally," said Sloan hastily.

"All the same, you'd better find out what the deceased wanted to see the University Chaplain about, Sloan, hadn't you?"

"Yes, sir."

"Now, if Hamlet had only got things straight in his own mind right at the very beginning . . ."

Sloan rang off as soon as he decently could.

*

The little group of dons that had foregathered in the Combination Room at Tarsus College had now moved into the Hall and taken their places at High Table. Their numbers did not compare with those present on the previous Tuesday evening, the first night of term—there were too many absentees for that. The Master of Tarsus, Kenneth Lorimer, was with the Vice-Chancellor: the news about Henry Moleyns and the sit-in had seriously up-staged his own recitation, rehearsed in the train, of how he had got the University Grants Committee round to his way of thinking, not easily, mind you, but after a struggle. . . .

Basil Willacy was at the sit-in, where he was—much to his annoyance—totally eclipsed by Professor Timothy Teed, who was there, too, and who for some reason best known to himself had adopted the rig-out favoured by his late Majesty King Edward the Seventh when out for a day's shooting at Sandringham. John Hardiman, the Bursar, hadn't felt like eating after seeing Henry Moleyns and—in between finding somewhere for what Detective Inspector Sloan bluntly called a murder headquarters and he himself still preferred to think of as an office—was fortifying himself with eggnog instead in his room. Hilda Linaker hadn't appeared either.

Professor Tomlin had led the way in. "It's my turn to say Grace, gentlemen. Do you think I should—ah—say anything else?"

There was a general shaking of heads. The dons were of one mind.

"No, no. . . ."

"The Master's job, don't you think?"

"Tomorrow would be better, surely. . . ."

"We don't really know enough to say anything, do we?"

"There's no one here, anyway," said the junior scientist. He, at least, was aware of the preternatural hush in the Hall. "Well, hardly anyone."

This was true. The High Table was not the only one to be seriously diminished in number. Beyond it, all the way to the Buttery, stretched tables almost empty of students. There was only one that was anything like full and that was the one nearest to the Buttery.

The dons peered round.

"Quite like *Zuleika Dobson*, isn't it?" said Neil Carruthers.

"You said you preferred the place without students, Tomlin," Bernard Watkinson reminded him. "Now you've got it that way. At a price, of course."

Professor McLeish adjusted his glasses. "There are some dining, you know."

"A handful of dissenters," suggested Roger Hedden, the sociologist. "I suppose I should be taking a professional interest in an out-group. The non-sitters-in or the sitters-out."

"They're scientists, I hope," said Mautby, still visibly seething about his violated laboratory. "If I find my ecologists haven't too much sense—and too much to do—for sit-ins, then I shall have something to say to them tomorrow."

"Plenty of politics in ecology," remarked Carruthers provocatively. "You've only got to call it 'food supply' instead and everyone starts getting excited."

"If they are my ecologists over there," said Mautby, "and I think they are—at least they're eating here properly and not camping in their rooms feeding out of tins of *Phaseolus vulgaris*."

"Of what?" asked old McLeish. Sanskrit—but little else— was an open book to him.

"The humble baked bean," explained Hedden kindly.

"Talking of food," said Watkinson, "I can see from here that Fat Boy hasn't gone to the sit-in."

"Talbot?" said Carruthers. "You won't catch him going anywhere that the food supply is restricted. Where's our doughty College Librarian, though?" He looked round the High Table. "He's not here. Don't say Pringle has defected to Malcolm Humbert's cause."

Professor Tomlin gave a short laugh. "No need to worry about that, Neil. He's an opportunist, is our Peter. He's taken advantage of the Greatorex's being closed today because of the sit-in and gone off to the Bodleian."

"Something they've got that we haven't?" enquired Watkinson slyly. "I thought the Greatorex was perfect."

"Only in certain fields, I understand," responded Tomlin gravely. He paused. "You know, I'm not at all sure that I shouldn't have mentioned poor Moleyns this evening after all. . . ." He was accountable nightly to his wife, the Bishop's daughter, as well as to the Master of Tarsus, and of the two she probed the more deeply.

"Don't worry," said Carruthers, the moral philosopher. "They know. You can't keep something like that quiet. And saying anything won't help." People expected philosophers to be comforters, but they weren't. On the contrary, in fact. Carruthers pointed to the table next to the Buttery. "See how quiet they are."

He was quite right. The man with the shoulder-length hair sitting half-way down the table—Barry Naismyth—was uncommonly subdued. So were the others there, all of them all too well aware of the empty chair in their midst—Henry Moleyns' chair.

"Polly?" asked Derek Doughty, unnaturally anxious. "Where's Polly? She wasn't going to go to the sit-in."

"She's seeing the police," said Martin Robinson. His father was on the Bench and approved of the police. He wondered how soon he would be on the telephone, too. . . .

"They came to the Madrigal and Glee Club," said Barry Naismyth, "and talked to Stephen Smithers."

"Stephen Smithers?" echoed Martin Robinson.

"He was the last to arrive, that's all," said Naismyth hastily. No one could seriously suspect Smithers of violence.

"And Colin?" asked Doughty, looking at the other empty chair. "Where's he?"

Tommy Talbot shook his head. "Nobody knows. They're looking for him everywhere." Unlike the Bursar, Talbot was still eating well. "The police want him to identify his things."

"That's a funny business, too," said Naismyth thoughtfully. "It doesn't make sense—someone nicking Colin's things, and then leaving them out by the fountain."

"Someone want me?" said Colin Ellison himself, suddenly appearing from behind them. "Sorry to be late again."

"Talk of the . . ." began Robinson, and stopped.

"Devil," Ellison finished pleasantly for him. "I wasn't going to come down to eat tonight but I was afraid you'd all think I was at the sit-in if I didn't." He pulled out a chair and sat down, looking round at the empty chairs as he did so. "Don't say Henry went after all? And Polly?"

"Haven't you heard?" responded Naismyth sharply.

It was soon obvious to them all—and to the police later—that Colin Ellison either really and truly hadn't heard about Henry Moleyns or was going to insist until kingdom come that he hadn't: which at this moment amounted to the same thing.

9

Counter-parry

Miss Hilda Linaker's set of rooms were pleasantly feminine in spite of her athletic appearance, and comfortably untidy. They were on the second floor of Tarsus College and in daylight must have commanded a fine view over the quadrangle. There were books everywhere. Detective Inspector Sloan was sitting in a fireside chair facing Miss Linaker. His only book was a notebook and it was open on his knee.

"I saw no evil," she said seriously, "and I heard no evil."

"You must have been very near," he said.

"Near in time and near in distance," she agreed in Aristotelian vein. "Twenty-six minutes past seven could easily have been the time we were there but, as I said before, I can't be quite sure."

"A pity it wasn't raining," he said involuntarily.

"Then you'd have known how long Colin Ellison's things had been out by the fountain, wouldn't you."

At least, thought Sloan, ready comprehension was to hand in a university setting. That, though, like much else, cut two ways. It meant that whoever he was dealing with in the way of a villain was likely to be clever, too. He asked her if she had seen anyone at all.

"Oh, yes," said the don, "there were quite a few people about. There always are round about the lodge and the quadrangle, and they weren't all at the sit-in. It's just that I didn't notice anyone in particular—except Polly Mantle, of course. I know most of the girls in Tarsus by sight even if I don't teach them."

"And Henry Moleyns?" asked Sloan. "Did you know him?"

"Not really," she replied, "but I happened to hear him arguing in the Library yesterday."

"Oh," said Sloan alertly. "Who with?"

The woman shook her head. "I don't know with whom. There were three of them, actually. You'd better ask Mr.

Hedden that. The men, I must say, I don't all know by sight unless they're my students. But Roger Hedden . . ."

"Hedden?"

"Lecturer in Sociology."

Sloan's professional mask must have slipped because Miss Linaker said quite gravely, "I believe he subscribes to Alexander Pope's view."

"And what would that be?" asked Sloan, out of his depth.

"That the proper study of mankind is man."

"Ah." There was another definition of a sociologist Sloan had seen somewhere . . . the police canteen, he thought. Someone had pinned it up after they'd had a visit from a postgraduate sociologist doing a thesis on something wildly improbable like "the influence of their working surroundings on policemen." How had it defined sociology? "The study of those who don't need studying by those who do." It had stayed up on the canteen wall a long time, had that one.

Miss Linaker was still speaking. "Roger Hedden must have seen to whom poor Moleyns was talking, Inspector, because he was so much nearer than I was. It was he who complained to me about the noise they were making. I knew that one of them was Moleyns only because he came over to Tarsus immediately afterwards to ask to see Professor Watkinson."

"Watkinson?" Sloan wrote that name down under Hedden's.

"Bernard Watkinson, Modern History," said Hilda Linaker.

Sloan was irresistibly reminded of Wales: Jones the Shop, Jones the Post, Jones the Railway. . . . Here at the University you weren't just a name but a name and a subject. That, he supposed, was one stage better than being a name and a number—as in the Army and the Police—and prison . . . or a name and a disease, as in hospital, which was worse.

Miss Linaker, who seemed to have an uncanny facility for following his mind, said, "We're all specialists here. That's our trouble. We all know too much about our own field and not enough about the next person's."

"It has its dangers," agreed Sloan moderately. The Superintendent, now—he discounted all expert opinion on principle—and, so they said, did juries. . . .

"The territorial imperative of learning, I suppose you could call it," said Miss Linaker, demonstrating that in universities, at least, trains of thought, once started, ran on.

Sloan didn't know whether to write that down or not.

"That," amplified Miss Linaker, "means 'Keep Off, It's Mine.'"

Now there was a sentiment every policeman understood. His own property was very dear to every normal citizen—dearer than his own person, often enough (perhaps they could explain that in a university)—and disregarding his rightful claims to that property, the basis of most crime. And if you didn't learn that early on, then you weren't going to make much of a policeman.

"They say it applies to animals, too," observed Miss Linaker, still keeping to the point. "I must say it's an unusual academic who ventures an opinion on something in someone else's field—except mine, of course," she added dryly. "Everyone feels qualified in English Literature."

"Quite so," said Sloan. After *Hamlet*, that certainly went for Superintendent Leeyes, too. "They tell me, miss, that you were wearing a gown."

"My working clothes, Inspector. Proclaiming to the world what I'm doing. Like 'Young Harry, with his beaver on.'"

"I see." He didn't, of course, so he looked down at his notebook and repeated, "'Professor Watkinson, Modern History.'"

"I don't know what it was that Moleyns wanted to see him about," said Miss Linaker. "You'll have to ask him that."

"Yes, indeed," said Sloan. "Now—er—miss—madam—perhaps you would be kind enough to tell me where you had come from. . . . I mean, from where had you come. . . ." Sloan hesitated. Even that didn't sound right and he ought to try to get it right here. What was it that their English master used to bawl at them so they would remember—only Sloan hadn't remembered—"A preposition is something you shouldn't end a sentence with." His intention was clear, that was what mattered. The Superintendent, that master of police English, said that grammar was only difficult when you thought about it. Mind you, the only grammatical point that was ever seriously considered down at the Police Station was that perennially knotty one about why men were hanged while game was hung. He would have liked to have asked the don that.

Instead he said, "I mean, before you met up with Polly Mantle."

"The Porter's Lodge," she said. "I'd been out in the town to see someone. I don't know if it matters who, but it was Mr.

Pringle, the Librarian. He was out—away, actually—so I came back."

*

It was Detective Constable Crosby who was interviewing Polly Mantle and he was enjoying every minute of it.

"There isn't a lot to tell, Officer," she told him.

"I'm sorry to hear that, miss," he said, settling himself comfortably into a chair. She really was a most attractive girl . . . and he liked being called "Officer."

"I was just coming back to my room, you see, when I happened to bump into Miss Linaker."

"Coming back where from?" asked Crosby who—university ambience or not—had ideas of his own on direct speech which were in no way dependent upon considerations of grammar.

"Let me see, now. . . ." An engaging dimple appeared as if of its own volition on each of Miss Mantle's nicely rounded cheeks. "It's been such a funny day what with the sit-in and everything."

"We need to know," said Crosby even more directly. "It might matter. Now."

"I'd been working in Bones and Stones," said the girl readily enough. "I really wanted to use the Library—I've got an essay for Mr. Mautby—but they'd closed it."

"I'm glad to hear it, miss."

"Are you? Why?"

"That's where the old gentleman's bust is, isn't it?"

"Jacob Greatorex?"

"The one with the chin and the long hair."

She nodded vigorously. "That's right. He looks like Charles the Second but firmer."

"We have found that the young gentlemen are inclined to use him as a mascot when they're excited." To hear him, anyone would think Crosby was old.

The dimples deepened. "I hadn't thought of that."

"And young gentlemen from other universities are in the habit of treating him as a trophy," said the constable prosaically. He wasn't old. It was just that he'd had to give up those sorts of games earlier than the undergraduates had.

"Ah, I see."

"We've had a lot of trouble with that bust down at the station."

"Have you?" she responded with lively sympathy.

"There was a raiding party from Oxford last year."

"I remember. After a Rugby match."

"Two breaches of the peace, one assault and one obstruction of the police in the execution of their duty," recited Crosby.

"Was that you?" she asked intuitively. She really was going to make someone a splendid wife one day.

The constable nodded and became a size larger at once. "And before that, miss, they came for it from one of the London Hospital Medical Schools. Very rough, the medical young gentlemen."

"I suppose it's because they're going to be doctors," said Polly.

"Two broken noses, four black eyes and a dislocated finger," tallied Crosby.

"Who won?" asked Polly.

"One nose was ours," said Crosby. The possessive plural clearly referred to the forces of law and order versus the rest. "The London lot caught most of the damage."

"Good for us," said Polly. Her plural pronoun equally rightly took in the University of Calleshire against the rest of the student world.

"They got as far as Calleford with the bust, though."

"Poor Jacob Greatorex."

"But we got it back," said Crosby. It was not at all clear this time whose achievement this was.

"Good for you," murmured Polly tactfully.

"So, miss, that's why they closed the Library."

"And that's why I had to go to Bones and Stones instead. And when they started to close up there," said Miss Mantle, "I came back to Tarsus."

"That would have been about . . . when?"

"I must have left about twenty past seven—it doesn't take more than a minute or two to get back from there, and then I saw Miss Linaker and we walked through the quad together and found all Colin's things by the fountain." She looked at him anxiously. "Does that help?"

"Not much," said Crosby.

*

Sloan caught up with Roger Hedden just as he was leaving the dining hall of Tarsus College. Professor Mautby was with him.

"Arguing in the Library, Inspector?" The sociologist gave a short laugh. "I'll say Moleyns was arguing. I was going to go over to stop them because they were making such a row."

"Them?"

"Ellison, who's supposed to be a pacifist, and Bennett," said Roger Hedden. "He was the other man. Hugh Bennett. I know him all right. He's one of my sociology students but Moleyns wasn't. I wouldn't have known who he was if he hadn't come over here afterwards asking for Professor Watkinson."

"Really, sir?" said Sloan mildly. "Was he an argumentative type, would you say?" Accidents going somewhere to happen, victims looking for someone to attack them, wars waiting for a trigger to tighten, fires only short of a match: that was how the experts in human behaviour thought these days.

Professor Mautby looked up at that. "I shouldn't have said so and as it happens I do know him—and Ellison, too, if it comes to that. Moleyns was reading ecology, you see."

"Quite," said Sloan. So far this—that he had been reading ecology—seemed all that he had been able to establish about the dead man.

"But," added Mautby, "I can tell you he did have another row the day before yesterday. On Tuesday evening. With a man called Challoner."

Hedden smiled thinly. "That's not difficult. Most people have a row with Michael Challoner sooner or later. He's that sort of man."

"Not at the very beginning of term, though, as a rule," pointed out Mautby. "They aren't usually quite so contentious early on."

"You don't say," murmured Sloan appreciatively. From what he had already heard so far at the University, Professor Simon Mautby's own fuse was the shortest of them all: arteries hardening while you looked at him.

"It was only the first night of term, remember, Inspector," the scientist said. "It's generally later that tempers begin to slip a bit."

"Slip a bit!" snorted Roger Hedden at his side. "That's putting Tuesday's row rather mildly, isn't it?"

"Is it?" Sloan encouraged the conversation, aware that at this stage anything—anything at all—might prove to be detective straw from which legal bricks could later be made: barristers were surprising brickmakers.

"Hammer and tongs weren't in it," said Hedden crisply, "and it was Moleyns whom Challoner was arguing with then."

Professor Mautby nodded confirmation of that. "I did detect atmospheric changes," he admitted.

Sloan had no difficulty in evaluating this. Like many other explosive personalities, Professor Mautby no doubt put other people's reactions on a level with his own: and they weren't. One man's apoplexy was another man's constraint.

"We heard them at High Table, Inspector," said Roger Hedden, "and believe you me, that takes a bit of doing these days. We very nearly had to have the row stopped, actually, and then the noise died down."

"There's no discipline left anywhere these days," lamented Mautby. "There's Moleyns lying dead, the Dean of Almstone prisoner in his own College of all things, the students arguing like so many fishwives. . . ."

"Your laboratory broken into," said Hedden. "And white mice where they shouldn't be."

Mautby didn't actually say that he didn't know what the world was coming to, but the sentiment was writ large upon his countenance.

"Moleyns," said Sloan, whose own remit was more specific, "what sort of a student was he?"

Professor Mautby shot Sloan a keen look. "Good without being inspired. Conscientious and all that. Kept up with his work all right."

Hedden leaned over and said gently, "All Mr. Mautby's students keep up with their work all right, Inspector."

Sloan could well believe this.

"They're here to work, Inspector," said Mautby shortly. "They shouldn't be here if they don't. Waste of the country's money."

"And Colin Ellison?" asked Sloan on an impulse. "He's one of yours, too, isn't he? What's he like?"

"Brilliant," said Mautby without hesitation. "One of the best men I've ever taught. Nothing run-of-the-mill about him—in spite of the pacifism."

Mautby would get on well with Superintendent Leeyes. If a man held different views from the Superintendent's own he stood condemned until proved otherwise.

Sloan made a note about Ellison. He didn't know the academic equivalent of topping the bill and having one's name up in lights at a university, but from the Professor's tone that was where Ellison was heading. He turned back to the lecturer in sociology. "Now, Mr. Hedden, I understand that when you saw Moleyns yesterday he was asking to see Professor Watkinson. Did he say what about?"

"Watkinson? No, I don't know—but look here, you could ask him yourself. There he is." Hedden pointed out the ascetic-looking man of about sixty with a head of grizzled grey hair who was coming out of the door from the dining hall. "Hey, Watkinson! The Inspector here wants to know when you saw Moleyns."

"I didn't." The Professor of Modern History acknowledged Sloan with a quick jerk of his head. "The young blighter didn't turn up."

"When should he have done?" enquired Sloan.

"I left him a note in his pigeon-hole telling him I'd see him in my rooms after I'd finished my tutorials at noon today."

"And?"

"And he didn't come."

"Or send a message?" asked Sloan quickly.

An ironic twist appeared on Watkinson's lips. "Stood me up as neatly as if he'd been a woman."

"And no apology afterwards?"

"My dear Inspector, that was yesterday. Today nobody apologises for anything. I just went on working." His tone changed. "Actually, I'm doing a paper on Stanley Baldwin's foreign policy. . . ."

Sloan cleared his throat. If there was one patch of British diplomatic history he didn't want to know about . . . one area where he felt veils should be drawn, not lifted aside . . . one time he thought that was better not remembered. . . .

"I've been working on the Cabinet papers," went on the historian, "and one or two quite interesting points have emerged. . . ."

His own father, Sloan remembered, hadn't even been able to remain coherent on the subject of Baldwin's foreign policy though he'd been more forgiving than was fashionable at the time about Neville Chamberlain—and more cynical about Russia, too. "These days," he said smoothly, "the young do rather expect you to wait upon their convenience."

Down at the station they said you even had to watch the police cadets now but he, Sloan, wouldn't know about that. They didn't often have trouble with them at Berebury: not

once they'd heard Superintendent Leeyes's introductory address on what was expected of a policeman. As soliloquies
went, there wasn't a lot in *Hamlet* to beat it.

Professor Mautby was frowning at Sloan's last remark about
impolite students. "I shouldn't have thought Henry Moleyns
was one of those. To me he seemed quite well-behaved.
Brought up by an aunt, I understand. That might make a
difference, of course."

Sloan thought it very likely. There was a certain detachment
about aunts.

"My dear Mautby," said Professor Watkinson in pained
tones, "do you know that the last time we had any trouble here
and I ventured an opinion on it, my students had the
effrontery to tell me that I was paid to teach them Modern
History and nothing else. I told them," he added spiritedly,
"that it was manners they needed to learn more than either
history or subversion, and it's still true."

"When did he make the arrangement to see you?" asked
Sloan, who was finding that a certain tenacity of purpose was
called for in questioning professors.

"Yesterday morning," said the historian promptly. "He
wanted to know if he could come and consult me about
something that was interesting him but that he didn't know
very much about. Makes a change," he said gruffly. "My own
students all think they know everything about history because
it's happened."

"Now, being a scientist," said Professor Mautby, "brings it
home to you how much you don't know. Besides"—he gave
something approaching a grin—"I keep telling them."

Sloan said to Professor Watkinson, "So Moleyns asked to see
you about something but didn't turn up?"

"Precisely. What about and why he didn't come I don't
know, and now, Inspector, I suppose we never shall."

Oh, yes, we will, decided Sloan vehemently.

But he did not say it aloud.

10

Straight Thrust

Aunts were different, all right. Sloan would have been prepared to admit that as soon as he set eyes on Miss Marion Moleyns. Maiden aunt she might be but she was certainly not the fussy, amiable, tearful, bootee-knitting, birthday-present-giving variety of aunt of popular imagination. Miss Moleyns was first and foremost a woman who worked for her living, and it showed. Dry-eyed, she confronted Sloan across the Bursar's desk.

"We always were an unlucky family," she said bleakly, "and this proves it, doesn't it?"

Sloan could only agree that it did.

"My brother and his wife were killed in a car crash, Inspector, and I don't reckon you can be unluckier than that, do you?"

Sloan could only agree that you couldn't. Traffic Inspector Harpe would be right behind him there.

"The boy was ten at the time," she said, in a remote way. "I've had him since then, you know."

"Yes," said Sloan gently.

"I must say he was very good at the time."

Sloan suspected that she meant by this—as most people do—that he had shown little emotion. "And since?" he asked, understanding that she was also telling him that she, too, equated "good" with reserve of feeling and wouldn't make a fuss now.

"No trouble." She inclined her head. "On his own a lot, of course."

"Naturally."

"I couldn't help that."

"No," agreed Sloan, well aware that one-parent families and their equivalent have never had it easy. The wonder was that a do-gooding society had taken so long to wake up to the fact. All working coppers found it out very early on.

Miss Moleyns was still talking. "I had a living to earn, you see." She tightened her lips. "Two livings, actually."

"Your brother . . ."

"My brother, Inspector, lived for the day and, believe me, his wife was no saver."

"I see." Sloan cleared his throat: however painful it was, their son's name was going to have to be recalled from the conversational limbo of the newly dead. "And Henry . . . what sort of a boy was Henry?"

"He was most thoughtful," she said detachedly. "Quite clever, the school said, though I must say I couldn't see why he wanted to do—what do they call it?—ecology. We weren't country people at all."

Sloan did not pursue this. Instead he enquired, "Girl friends?"

Miss Moleyns shook her head. "Nobody special that I knew about," she said. "The odd name cropped up but never more than once or twice."

Miss Moleyns was clearly not a Wodehouse-type aunt.

"Of course," she went on, "he'd have had to finish at University and get a job before he could think of marrying."

Miss Moleyns was even more clearly quite out of touch with her nephew's generation—if not with her nephew. Little things like being able to afford it no longer seemed to deter the young. . . .

"This summer," he prompted her. "What had he been doing?"

"He picked fruit at first," she said, "to earn some money. He was saving up. He wanted one of those student railway tickets—you know—the go-anywhere ones."

Sloan nodded. You couldn't go anywhere with them; of course. Not yet. That Foreign Secretary's dream after the war . . . who had it been now? . . . of going to Victoria and buying a ticket for where the 'ell you liked . . . Ernest Bevin, that had been his name . . . hadn't come true yet. Though he'd been talking about passports, not railway tickets.

"At least," said Marion Moleyns tonelessly, "he'd had his holiday before . . . before . . ."

"Where did he go?"

"All sorts of places," she said vaguely. "Belgium . . . I know he went there because he told me they hadn't got any hedges."

"Poor little Belgium." Now whereabouts in his subconscious had that come from?

"And flat?"

"Very flat, Belgium," said Sloan. Or that?

"Like Norfolk, Henry said it was."

Of course. That was where that had come from.

"Waterloo wasn't like what Henry had expected, though."

"Where else did he go?" asked Sloan, deciding that this was no occasion for quoting the Duke of Wellington.

"I had a picture postcard from Cologne," she said.

A young man going east, decided Sloan to himself.

"It was of the Cathedral," said Miss Moleyns. "Very pretty—quite English in a way."

This, Sloan was aware, was praise indeed. "What did he say on the card?"

"That I wouldn't like the food there," she said simply.

Henry Moleyns, then, hadn't wasted his time on the "wish you were here" style of platitude. Nor his money on a Donald McGill-type card.

"All that red cabbage," she said.

"Quite," said Sloan. Of such stuff are xenophobes made.

"Not," she added literally, "that I would have liked a bicycle tour with a tent either but . . . but . . . but I would have liked to have had his last few weeks with him if only I'd known."

Sloan nodded. It was a constant refrain where there was a sudden death. Perhaps the saving grace of terminal illness was that this feeling was spared those around the deceased.

Miss Marion Moleyns looked straight across the Bursar's desk at Sloan in that curious mixture of attitude compounded of the defensive and the aggressive of one for whom life has never been easy. "He was a good boy, you see, Inspector. And what I want to know," she demanded, a harsher note creeping into her voice, "is why anyone would want to do a thing like this to him?"

"And that," answered Sloan in the same spirit, "I can't tell you yet—but I will, I can promise you. Just give me a little time."

*

When Detective Inspector Sloan next saw Crosby he was approaching the fountain and the constable was crossing the

Tarsus College quadrangle with a steaming jug of coffee in one hand and in the other two cups, one on top of the other, and balanced on top of those a plate with some sandwiches on it. The sandwiches were perilously crowned with a salt cellar.

Sloan regarded his subordinate for a long moment and then said sardonically, "And for your next trick?"

"I wasn't absolutely sure what a College Buttery was," said Crosby virtuously, "so I went to find out." He cast an anxious glance at the salt cellar, which was wobbling as uncertainly as a Balkan throne. "Sir, do you think we could sit down by the fountain?"

As they settled themselves on the parapet Sloan looked at his watch. He would telephone his wife next to say that he wouldn't be home before morning. She wouldn't mind. Or if she minded she wouldn't say. It was one of the things she was used to. And if, when it came, the new baby cried in the night she knew she would have to soothe it alone. The first nursery rhyme that any detective's child learnt was ` "Bye, baby bunting, Father's gone a-hunting. . . ."

"The man Colin Ellison," said Crosby basely dividing the sandwiches on a purely mathematical basis and without any regard to rank, "says he doesn't know anything about anything."

"He was part of the great row in the library," said Sloan, "his room was robbed, and for my money he was somewhere he shouldn't have been yesterday evening."

"He says he didn't even know Moleyns was dead until he got to the dining hall this evening."

"And," added Sloan, "he was around here about the time Moleyns bought it. Or so Sneezy says."

"Sneezy, sir? Oh, yes, our Stephen Smithers."

"*Snow White and the Seven Dwarfs*," said Sloan crisply. "Before your time, Crosby."

"Yes, sir."

Now he came to think about it, you could get wall-papers with the nicer characters from the rich store of English fairy tales printed on them especially for children's nurseries. They, he and Margaret, would have to think about having that—nothing frightening, of course, but enough pictures for the baby to build fantasies of its own around.

"Coffee," said Crosby, unwittingly interrupting a vision which was a confusion of fairy-tale castles and knights in shining armour that would have greatly surprised him had he been able to share it. "They," he went on, "were Colin Ellison's things all right, sir. He checked them through quite carefully for me just now."

"All present and correct?"

"Nothing missing—he was sure about that—and nothing damaged that he could see."

"And no fingerprints either, I take it?"

"No, sir. It doesn't make sense."

"It will," said Sloan rather wearily, "in the end. So will Moleyns' wanting to see the Chaplain when we find out what all that caper was about." He bit into a sandwich. "Tell me, Crosby, why should a man of that age want to see a chaplain?"

Crosby frowned. "About getting married, sir, would you think?"

"Married?" grunted Sloan. "I hadn't thought of that."

"It wouldn't be a christening," continued the constable, in whose family circle the Church featured in Rites of Passage on wheels and nothing else, "would it, now?"

"Why not?" asked Sloan, intrigued. "Even students . . ."

"If it was a christening," pronounced Crosby, "the mother would lay it on, wouldn't she?"

"I wouldn't know about that," murmured Sloan. And he didn't either. Not yet. But soon he would be learning. "And," he added curiously, "how are you so sure?"

"My sisters," said Crosby bashfully. "Always making an uncle of me, they are."

Sloan tried to visualize a neat and tidy Crosby standing near the font with a white bundle in his arms, failed—and helped himself to another sandwich. "Assuming," he said with heavy irony, "that the marriage service is out and that christenings are women's work"—fatherhood was going to be a new experience for Sloan; he obviously had a lot to learn—"what else do you think Moleyns might have wanted to consult a chaplain about?"

"I couldn't say, sir, I'm sure."

"What sort of problem would you consult a chaplain about?" asked Sloan, changing his tack slightly. After all, Crosby couldn't be that much older than all these undergraduates— and everyone couldn't be of the same simple faith as the Superintendent.

"Getting married," said Crosby without hesitation.

"You've got a one-track mind," snapped Sloan.

"Yes, sir." He coughed and tried again. "Perhaps Henry

Moleyns had been and gone and done something that he shouldn't have done, then."

"Confession? That's a thought." Sloan had seen many men weighed down with guilt in his time, a prison sentence a welcome expiation in spite of what the reformers said.

Crosby lifted his coffee cup. "You usually want to tell somebody if you've blotted your copy-book, sir, don't you?"

"That's just as well, too," said Sloan flatly, "otherwise there would be a sight fewer cases solved."

"Course, he might just have had a simple problem about what to do about something," ventured Crosby.

"He was going to see Professor Watkinson, too, and he's a historian."

"A historical problem, then," said Crosby obligingly.

"That reminds me." Sloan flipped over the pages of his notebook. "The Professor said that he sent him a note."

"It's not in his room."

"Now, there's a thing," said Detective Inspector Sloan absently. "Make a note about that. . . ."

*

"I'v got the Berebury and District General Hospital on the line," announced Higgins, the porter, who was manning the Tarsus switchboard, "with a call for Detective Inspector Sloan. A Dr. Dabbe."

"Put him through," said Sloan.

The Bursar of Tarsus had found him a room at the opposite side of the quadrangle—"murder headquarters" seemed to Sloan an improbable description of it. The room belonged to a don of Tarsus presently enjoying a sabbatical year in the United States and was furnished with modern prints by De Chirico. He had only half an eye for them, which was just as well: he had a feeling that closer examination might not be a good thing. The bookcases, too, were full of books that Sloan would not have liked his wife to read.

But what worried him most of all was the white carpet. In Sloan's milieu carpets were for covering floors serviceably. This one was not only white but slightly fluffy and he didn't see how it could stay white for very long while the room doubled as a working place for a Scene of Crime Officer. The only comfort was that John Hardiman had asssured him that the owner would not be back for a year.

"That you, Sloan? Dabbe here."

There wouldn't be any carpets where Dr. Dabbe was ringing from, Sloan knew that. Only a stout composition floor hosed down a dozen times a day. And there were no prints hanging on the wall, except perhaps X-ray ones.

"This post mortem," began the pathologist.

"Yes, Doctor." Sloan pulled his notebook towards him.

"The deceased was a young man of average build—about twenty years old—you've got his exact age, I expect—properly nourished. . . ."

Pathologists had hobby-horses, too, and obesity was one of Dr. Dabbe's. He was always having a go at Sergeant Gelven—seventeen stone without his whistle—about his weight. "See you soon," was his favourite form of greeting to the portly detective, "on my slab." He would chide the too thin, also, but not so often.

". . . and quite muscular," went on Dr. Dabbe now.

"He'd been on a bicycle tour," Sloan informed him absently, "so he would be."

"Had he? Well, there were certainly no signs of disease present. The cause of death was a penetrating wound between the fourth rib and the fifth rib just to the left of the sternum."

"Missing the bone?" said Sloan.

"It isn't bone there," said Dabbe. "Only cartilage. Bony rib doesn't start until another inch each side of the breastbone."

"Missing the cartilage, then," said Sloan patiently.

"That sort of wound is almost always going to miss the cartilage," said the pathologist. "Most things coming up against it are going to be deflected either above or below the rib and through the intercostal muscles."

"Are they?" said Sloan non-committally.

"If you think of your ribs as being like Venetian blinds on edge you can see that anything pointed at them would stand a good chance of getting through, can't you?"

"Yes," said Sloan. "What we need to know, though, is—"

"The wound," went on the pathologist, equally undeflected, "extends through the pericardium and the anterior wall of the left ventricle."

"Which means . . ." said Sloan gamely.

"I opened the pericardial sac, of course," said Dr. Dabbe, not listening.

"Of course," murmured Sloan.

"Naturally it was full of blood."

Noises of agreement seemed called for, so Sloan made them.

"And the subject was standing up."

"Was he?" said Sloan. He didn't know how much that information was going to help him, but he wrote it down.

"As Vespasian said," remarked Dr. Dabbe.

"Who?"

"Vespasian. He was a Roman emperor who held that emperors should die standing up."

"Did he?" said Sloan.

"Vespasian? No, come to think of it, I don't believe he did. Died in his bed."

Sloan took a deep breath. "And Henry Moleyns?"

"He nearly did," said Dr. Dabbe cheerfully. "There's a trickle of blood down the outside of the skin under the fourth intercostal space to prove it."

"That's something, I suppose," said Sloan, who had not for one moment lost track of the things he wanted to know. "Now, Doctor, about the weapon. . . ."

"Sharp, of course. It went through his clothes, too."

"Yes."

"Thin. Eight millimetres at the outside."

Sloan wrote that down, too. Not that he liked metric measurements. Oh, he understood them all right, and in theory they made adding up easier, but he still couldn't—what was the word they used these days?—he couldn't conceptualise them. Now, inches and yards he could imagine, and if anyone mentioned miles he knew where he was at once. The new baby would be all right. He'd never learn anything else.

"And not less than six point five," continued the pathologist.

"Six point five," echoed Sloan.

"Measure twice and cut once, as my old granny's dressmaker used to say, Sloan."

"Yes, Doctor." Dr. Dabbe always took an incorrigibly light-hearted view of his work. Perhaps it was the only way. Perhaps it was because pathologists were insulated from their patients in a way that other doctors weren't by death and—by custom—they never saw relatives anyway. That would have suited Sloan, too. It was when you saw the relatives that you saw crime as the pebble in the pond—the ripples reaching out further and further, lapping up the quiet by-waters of other people's lives. Drowning them sometimes, too.

"The sizes of the holes in the clothes, the skin and the visceral and parietal edges of the pericardium are all very much the same," carried on the pathologist, "so whatever the instrument was, it doesn't appreciably thicken up for the first part of its length."

"Amazing what you can tell from a hole," remarked Sloan, "isn't it?"

"I haven't finished," said Dabbe. "There's something else."

"The angle?" hazarded Sloan after a quick think.

"The angle was very interesting, Sloan."

"Not an upward thrust, then?" Upward thrusts were what they usually had on Saturday nights outside the pubs at the railway end of the town.

"Almost dead straight."

"That's odd."

"There was something else," said Dabbe.

"What was that?"

"The depth."

"What was so odd about that?"

"It wasn't too deep," said Dabbe slowly; "or too shallow."

"But just right?" There had been an advertisement once, surely. . . .

"Exactly right," said Dr. Dabbe, totally serious now. "So exactly right, Sloan, that whoever caused it either got everything spot on just by accident or . . ."

"Or," finished Sloan for him, choosing his words with care, "it was a highly skilled job."

"Very," agreed the pathologist. "By someone who'd done it before or been taught how. Sleep well, old chap."

11

One—Two

He did not sleep well. He was not the only one.

There were other people destined to have an unquiet night at the University of Calleshire as well as Detective Inspector Sloan. All might have seemed outwardly serene but all was by no means still. For one thing, events of the day were being

brought to the official notice of various highly-placed persons
in the county.

The Vice-Chancellor, duly apprised by the Bursar of the true
seriousness of the situation, saw his own duty as happily clear.
He at once passed the buck upwards in two directions—
spiritual and temporal.

He telephoned the Bishop's Palace first.

"My Lord . . ."

The Bishops of Calleford had by long custom held the
position of University Visitor. The present incumbent heard
the news from the Vice-Chancellor and offered appropriate
words of comfort as befitted his office but nevertheless
included the third Psalm—"Lord, how are they increased that
trouble me!"—in his own devotions that night.

The Vice-Chancellor politely acknowledged the words of
comfort, though they were likely to avail him little against the
strictures of either the national press or the University
Senate—the Scylla and Charybdis of his life—and it was not
accidental that he put Scylla first. He rang off and telephoned
the University Chancellor, the Duke of Calleshire, at Calle
Castle.

"Your Grace . . ."

At other less pressing moments the Vice-Chancellor was
wont to ponder exactly why custom and usage demanded that
he address two such eminently different characters—albeit
each of them in his own way exalted—by archaic forms of
address that seemed to have got themselves transposed.

His Grace the Duke of Calleshire fortunately considered
over-reaction to be the mark of Common Man and took the
news calmly enough. As a father of six he was in any case by
now pretty well inured to the shocks that youth can inflict
upon the middle-aged. He at first took an eighteenth-century
view of the cause. "Some girl, I suppose. . . ."

Police Superintendent Leeyes, one eye on the clock and
more experienced in having to wake people when the night
was really advanced, also decided to put his own superior in
the picture at a relatively decent hour. He put in a call to the
Assistant Chief Constable: like the Vice-Chancellor, keeping
the problem within the family but going upwards.

"At the University of Calleshire, sir," said Leeyes grittily.
There were no problems of title and mode of address here.

"Ah, yes. In Berebury."

"That's right." The Superintendent let out a sigh of relief. At least the Assistant Chief Constable (Magdalen College, Oxford, as well as the police one) wasn't going to pretend not only that he'd never heard of the University of Calleshire—a lot of people did that—but also that there were only two universities in England, one of which he'd been to. A lot more people did that.

"A sharp instrument, did you say? More of that about these days than there used to be." There were no words of comfort from this quarter. Only a completely professional view. "At least," he qualified this, "the Home Office statisticians say there are, and they should know, I suppose."

"And what is there less of, then, sir?"

"Still looking on the bright side, Superintendent?"

"They say," replied Leeyes without conviction, "that every cloud has a silver lining."

"Blunt instruments haven't gone up much. Not as a means of killing, anyway." With the prerogative of high authority he changed the subject abruptly. "What about the sit-in?"

"Still going on."

*

That was the point in time at which Detective Inspector Sloan managed to get through on the telephone to Superintendent Leeyes with Dr. Dabbe's report.

"He said what?" demanded the Superintendent explosively.

"That whoever stabbed Moleyns knew exactly what he was doing."

For once his superior responded with total silence.

"Down to the last centimetre," added Sloan weakly—finding to his surprise that Leeyes's silences were more unnerving than his peppery utterances.

"There's something going on there," said Leeyes at last—and profoundly.

"It does put a different face on things, sir, doesn't it?" agreed Sloan.

"Call it a new dimension," said Leeyes, who had once struggled through the opening chapter of Mr. J. W. Dunne's well-known work, *An Experiment with Time*.

"An experienced killer," mused Sloan. They didn't get many of those in Calleshire.

"In our manor," said Leeyes. "Ay, there's the rub."

"Beg pardon, sir?"

"*Hamlet.*"

"Oh."

"Science," announced Leeyes suddenly.

"Sir?"

"They do science there, don't they?"

"There are a lot of laboratories and things around," said Sloan vaguely.

"Then I reckon there's something going on there," said Leeyes again.

"Someone did let some white mice out," remembered Sloan. "Yesterday. If yesterday was Wednesday . . ." De Chirico's metaphysical paintings were unnerving things to have on the wall of a living room. Distracting wasn't in it. The only one that he thought he could understand was the print nearest to the telephone and that looked to him like Harlequin and Columbine. There had been a police pantomime for the kids once at Christmas with Harlequin and Columbine in it—with Harlequin bent on frustrating the knavish tricks of the Clown who was in love with Columbine. A proper police set-up that had been—plot and all, now he came to think of it—with Woman Police Constable Perkins—Pretty Polly—as Columbine, a tall lad with good legs from Traffic Division as Harlequin—not that Columbine's legs hadn't been good too, they had—and a crafty-looking type from Plain-clothes Division as the Clown. He'd have to brush up on pantomimes too now, with the baby coming—next year would be too soon, of course; it wouldn't be old enough—but after that . . .

"Experiments," Leeyes was declaring firmly, "that's what they've got the white mice for."

Sloan gritted his teeth. Even Crosby wouldn't have supposed Professor Mautby was keeping white mice in his laboratory as pets. Not knowing Professor Mautby, that is. The students were another matter. He wouldn't be too unbearably surprised from the look of them if one or two had their teddy bears up with them.

"Research," Leeyes said. "They do research in universities sometimes, Sloan, don't they?" He remembered the Assistant Chief Constable and qualified this. "In some universities, anyway."

"I wouldn't know, sir, except for the white mice."

"If," said Leeyes tartly, "it's the sort of research that involves people getting killed in the practised fashion that Dr. Dabbe suggests—"

"He only said—"

"Then," swept on Leeyes regardless, "no one's going to know except whoever's paying for it."

"The government, do you mean, sir?" asked Sloan, trying not to sound too obtuse.

"As long as it's our own government," said Leeyes piously, "and not someone else's, then that's what I do mean."

"How do we find out?"

"Ah," said Leeyes grandiosely, "that's a different matter. The forces of law and order on the ground are never told anything by government until the cat's out of the bag and someone wants somebody caught. Not that one half of the government ever knows what the other half's up to anyway."

"Yes, sir." Parliamentarians—like everyone else—haggled over the price of bicycle sheds, not what was going on inside defence contracts—in public, that is. As for the research being done for someone else's government . . .

"Universities," said Leeyes didactically, "are hotbeds of dissent. You've only got to read the newspapers . . ."

"Yes, sir."

"To say nothing of things like this sit-in," growled Leeyes. "Students are always agin the government."

"Yes, sir," said Sloan. His father used to go on about that. Something about their having been agin the government in Stanley Baldwin's time, too, that his father had brooded on at Munich and afterwards: "That this House will in no circumstances fight for King and country." "Doesn't mean much, sir," he said reassuringly. "The only thing that's different is that nowadays, as well as the students, some of the lecturers are against the government too."

Police Superintendent Leeyes said something distinctly unparliamentary about dissenting lecturers that would have pained those highly-educated souls had they been privileged to overhear it.

"Yes, sir," said Sloan automatically, "but where does that get us over this research business?"

"Man-eating mice?"

"Professor Mautby," said Sloan a trifle stiffly, "is an ecologist."

"Man-eating plants, then," responded Leeyes upon the instant.

Suddenly De Chirico's metaphysical prints seemed ordinary

and familiar while more terrifying visions as yet uncharted by artists drifted through Sloan's mind.

"Popular with the Treasury, of course," said Leeyes.

"Sir?"

"Saves ammunition. You should have seen them dole it out before Walcheren. . . ."

The seaborne landings at Walcheren had been the highlight of Superintendent Leeyes's war-time career. They came into the conversation on the slightest pretext—not for one moment did Sloan suppose that the wherewithal of war had really been in short supply there.

"Professor Mautby might be doing some work on plant-borne diseases," suggested Sloan hastily. Reminiscence had to be stemmed at least once a month.

"Germ warfare with a difference?" mused Leeyes, considering this.

"Buy your own seeds?" suggested Sloan lightly: the further they moved from Walcheren the better.

"You never know what scientists will get up to next," said Leeyes darkly. "Two-headed dogs . . ."

"Making two ears of corn grow where one had grown before . . ." began Sloan. No, that wasn't science: that was politics, he was sure.

"Instant villain cure," said Leeyes revealingly. "Perhaps they're working on that."

"It's what we want," Sloan endorsed this.

"Some of that *Alice in Wonderland* stuff," said Leeyes.

"Sir?"

"One dose and they grow smaller."

That was something else Sloan would have to bone up on for his son. Inexplicably *Alice in Wonderland* had grown in importance over the years. He didn't know, though, that he would ever be able to explain "Jabberwocky."

"That's the idea, sir," he said heartily. "Smaller villains." Actually, petty criminals were usually small men, anyway, and on the undernourished side too. Or was it just that policemen and prison officers were big ones by comparison? They said small people were more highly sexed than tall ones—perhaps a tendency to crime went that way too. That was a nice point for the moralists. . . .

"'Let me have men about me that are fat,'" said the Superintendent in his quoting voice.

"*Hamlet?*" hazarded Sloan. If it wasn't Walcheren it would be *Hamlet* these days.

"*Julius Caesar,*" said Leeyes. "Where is all this getting us, Sloan?"

"Nowhere, sir. All that Henry Moleyns has done so far that we know about is duck out of the sit-in, probably nick some things from the boy Ellison's room . . ."

"And leave them where we were bound to find them."

"Have a row with another student, Hugh Bennett."

"Which may or may not mean anything," said Leeyes.

"Make—and break—an appointment with the Professor of Modern History."

"But about what we don't know," said Leeyes with scant regard for syntax.

Sloan hadn't finished. "Make—and not be able to keep—an appointment with the Chaplain."

Leeyes hadn't finished either. "And get himself killed," he said.

"That, too," agreed Sloan as he rang off.

He paused by the print on the wall that had seemed to him like Columbine and Harlequin and read the caption for the first time. It said "Hector and Andromache." He turned off the light and stepped out of the room. He hadn't time for the ancient Greeks just now.

12
———————

Counter-Riposte

Detective Inspector Sloan began his night round with a visit to the University Sanatorium.

It was a curious Victorian building—midway in architectural style between Fairfax and Ireton Colleges and the university's two modern ones. The edifice owed its position—isolated from all other College buildings—to what was known to medical science about infectious diseases at the time it was built, and its design to the influence of William Butterfield and his Keble College at Oxford.

Matron lived in the building in similarly splendid isolation. As it happened, this nicely reflected her situation among the academic community. Being both properly qualified for her job (at one of the oldest teaching hospitals) and a member of a noble profession, there were some social activities from which she could not very well be excluded and some (notably those involving good provender) from which she would not.

"On the other hand, she is not a member of this University," sticklers for College etiquette would insist to the Bursar when the smaller invitation lists were being compiled.

"Governesses used to exist in the same sort of no man's land," a social historian had once informed him unhelpfully.

"Neither one thing nor the other." One of the philosophers picked up the conversation. "Incidentally, that is one of the most interesting of theoretical propositions because if one is not one thing, logically one is something else. Plato said . . ."

On the whole the Bursar found they got on better when Plato was left out of discussions.

"Perhaps," another learned voice had suggested, "we should regard her as a Liberal Unionist."

There had been a pause, then:

"Ah," with satisfaction, "Oscar Wilde."

"'Oh, they count as Tories.'" Someone supplied the rest of the quotation in a Lady Bracknell voice. "'They dine with us. Or come in the evening at any rate.'"

"Neither flesh, fowl, nor good red herring. . . ."

The Bursar, John Hardiman, mindful of much co-operation in the matter of the emergency use of sanatorium beds late at night, would outwardly concur but later consult the good lady in question on the more germane matter of whether or not she wanted to come.

All that Detective Inspector Sloan knew about Matron was her ready acceptance of his bizarre proposals about the use of her sanatorium tonight. There had been nothing equivocal about her response to those—she had been as practical as Florence Nightingale at Scutari. He set off towards the sanatorium confident that she at any rate would have done her part.

Nevertheless he approached the building with circumspection and stood in the darkness of the University grounds until he could make out the other watchers. Even then he made no move, mindful of some highly idiosyncratic advice that he had once had from the Assistant Chief Constable. His mannered voice came unbidden now into Sloan's mind: "Never put up a bird, Inspector, until you're ready to shoot it."

The Assistant Chief Constable's analogies were all taken from the world of huntin', shootin' and fishin'. What was so interesting was the way in which they fitted so well into the world of thief-taking. Sloan glanced about him. Perhaps someone in the darkened campus which surrounded him was already writing a thesis on this.

It did not take him long to spot the watchers by the threshold. There was a whiff of tobacco smoke in the late evening air that betrayed the general direction of Police Constable Smith. Smith would not be the first person to be given away by my lady nicotine—she was as wayward a mistress as any of her sex. There was no tell-tale glow in the darkness, so Smith had either heard Sloan coming or perfected the art of invisible smoking. One of the first things a man learnt on the beat was the cupped hand, the swallowed smoke. . . .

Over on the other side of the path Police Constable Carpenter trod on a twig. Sloan could make out his outline against a bush.

"Dogberry and Verges," the Superintendent had said when he sent them over. "They can be your officers of the watch, and Heaven help the lot of you if anyone lays a finger on Battling Bertha." He had paused and added thoughtfully, "And Heaven help them, too, of course."

Sloan had taken his point.

When he had first asked for a woman police officer for the Moleyns case the Superintendent had taken it for granted that he would want Policewoman Perkins—people usually did want Policewoman Perkins. Not for nothing was she known affectionately throughout the Calleshire force as Pretty Polly. The County's other woman police constable was known, equally affectionately, as Battling Bertha.

True, motorists disadvantaged at being found in the wrong had been known to refer to her less affectionately. Shouts of "Seig Heil" had been heard in Berebury High Street and muttered references to "Fascists" in the more restrained atmosphere of the Crown Court—though one youth who had succumbed to the temptation offered when she had stooped to attend to a shoelace in Berebury's shopping precinct had to be hurriedly let off with a caution by a Bench in very real danger of losing its self-control.

Sloan had wanted Battling Bertha because she looked more

like Bridget Hellewell than Polly Perkins did: that was all, not because Polly Perkins wasn't as good at looking after herself as Battling Bertha. Many a man had attacked Polly in a lonely spot on a dark night only to find himself pinned to the ground until he was arrested. But there could be no confusing Polly's features with the raw-boned earnest ones of Bridget Hellewell, student leader.

And with a deep conscientious fervour Sloan hoped that Battling Bertha's homely features would do, and would not be injured in the process.

He moved over to Carpenter, giving Smith the chance to extinguish whatever he had been smoking. "All quiet?" he asked softly.

"Not a dicky-bird anywhere near, sir. Matron's gone to bed. She went up at her usual time, just as we arranged. Bathroom light out first, then her bedroom one. Ten minutes after that the other bedroom light, like you said."

"Who's up there with her?"

"Police Constable Baynes is in the bedroom and P. C. Collet is downstairs but out of sight." Carpenter tapped his pocket. "We've got all our signals laid on if anyone shows up."

"But nothing has so far?"

"Nothing near the sanatorium."

"What does that mean?"

"There's been someone over by Tarsus."

"Someone?" queried Sloan sharply. Carpenter should know better than this.

"A woman, sir."

"What doing?"

"Pacing up and down. At least, that's what it looked like from here. It's a tidy distance, sir, and it's pretty dark."

"Where exactly?" demanded Sloan. It was like drawing teeth, extracting information from Carpenter.

"This side of the Tarsus quadrangle."

All the Berebury Force used the word in full: always had. "Quad" sounded like something very different to a policeman, and they couldn't be doing with confusion.

Carpenter hastened on. "This side of the main building. It was only when she crossed in front of the entrance that you could see that there was anyone there at all. There's a little bit of light spilling out from that lamp above the entrance."

Sloan turned to look for himself.

"You've got to step into the light, sir, if you're going that way."

"And which way was she going?" asked Sloan, trying not to make his patience sound elaborate. That never got you anywhere with anybody.

"Nowhere," said Carpenter, contriving to sound injured. "Like I said, sir, that was the funny thing. She was just pacing up and down."

"Height?"

"Shortish."

"Fat or thin?" If a silhouette could convey anything, it was that.

"Plumpish."

"Anything else about her?"

Carpenter paused. "Not young," he said at last. "I think."

"We're getting on," conceded Sloan.

"Yes, sir."

"Clothes?"

"I couldn't rightly see, sir. I should say she had a coat on but I couldn't swear to it."

"I see." That was another thing that sorted out policemen from the rest of the world: the likelihood of having to swear on oath to whatever it was they said. "She's not there now, is she?"

And that, thought Sloan to himself fairly, was as silly a remark as any that poor Carpenter was likely to make. Superintendent Leeyes would compare Sloan with Horatio asking the nightwatchmen at Elsinore if Hamlet's father's ghost was still around on the battlements.

"No, sir," replied Carpenter, who, if asked a silly question, still answered it.

"Right," said Sloan more peaceably. "Now, remember what you're to do. . . ."

The trouble with both the Superintendent and his preoccupation with Hamlet, Prince of Denmark, was that they got into everything.

*

Higgins, the porter on the Tarsus gate, was having quite a struggle with one member of the University. Only the knowledge that his orders came from the Master of Tarsus in person strengthened his arm.

"No one is to come into the College tonight, Professor, without I let Dr. Lorimer know."

"Much too late to trouble him," said Simon Mautby with his customary firmness. "I'm only going across to my rooms for a moment. I'll lock up behind me, don't you worry about that."

That wasn't what Higgins was worried about but he didn't say so to Professor Mautby.

"An experiment," said the ecologist breezily. "Needs a special time-setting. I won't be long, Higgins. Time you shut up shop anyway, isn't it? All our late birds should be back in the nest by now, surely?"

"Most of them," said Higgins feelingly, "are still over at the sit-in at Almstone. I'm keeping open in case they aren't."

"Serve 'em right if they are locked out." Professor Mautby jangled his keys and set off through the Tarsus quadrangle. "Don't you lock me in, Higgins, either. That would never do. I've got work to do at home tonight."

*

Detective Inspector Sloan shook *Hamlet* out of his mind by walking across to the administration building at Almstone to check on the sit-in for himself.

There had been no change in personnel there. Other people—and other ranks—were permitted to show tiredness, battle-fatigue, even, but not men who were or had been sergeant-majors in the British Army. Alfred Palfreyman, presently Head Porter at Almstone College, but first and foremost sometime of the East Calleshire Regiment, looked in just as good trim now as he had looked that moment many, many hours ago when he had first come on duty.

Whether he had in fact snatched some sleep Sloan couldn't begin to guess: it might only have been that he could rest awake, as generations of recruits were led to believe, or perhaps that sergeant-majors needed no sleep—as Her Majesty's enemies were encouraged to think. In any event the secret of his untiring strength belonged with the other secrets of his profession, and the policeman, who had his own survival methods, secret to his own calling, invoked when life—or death—became too pressing, wouldn't have presumed to question him about it.

He greeted Sloan as an ally.

It was a nice point. The relationship between the Army—

the military power—and the Police—the civil power—has
traditionally been a delicate one. Indeed, the quality of the
relationship was often a factor in revolutions in Ruritanian
countries—banana republics couldn't always afford a police
force—but there was no room for doubt in Alfred Palfreyman's
mind about where either stood. The Army was there to protect
Queen and Country; the Police to preserve the Queen's Peace
and to protect the law-abiding. He saw Justice as clearly as did
the Lady with the Scales at the Old Bailey as having a duty to
"Defend the Children of the Poor and Punish the Wrong-
doer."

"Where will all this end?" he demanded of Sloan. "That's
what I want to know. First you have your student power and
now they want pupil power. . . ."

"Pram rule?" suggested Sloan lightly, though he was certain
that there was going to be none of that in his own house, come
the arrival of the new baby.

"Anarchy, more like," said Palfreyman. "Just you wait.
They'll need the Army again then. Any rule's better than no
rule, you know."

"The students . . ." said Sloan, ducking out of debate on
this. How not to argue was lesson one at some police training
schools. "The students. You've got them bottled up nicely for
us."

"No trouble," said Palfreyman with a deprecating wave of
the arm towards the administration block. He grinned a bit.
"Like our old grenade instructor used to say, they're only
dangerous until you know they're dangerous—then they're
safe."

"This boy Moleyns," said Sloan. "Anything funny about
him?"

"He wasn't a gentleman's gentleman, if that's what you
mean," said the Head Porter sagaciously. "Our trouble here is
that they're all looking more like each other every day."

"Unisex," pronounced Sloan.

"What they want to do," said Palfreyman, and not for the
first time, "is to get their hair cut."

"Yes," said Sloan. He, too, had heard that before. You would
have thought that every Magistrate that ever was had been
hand-reared on the legend of Samson and Delilah.

"Queen's Regulations," prescribed Palfreyman. "Now, if
they all stuck to those there'd be no trouble anywhere."

"Quite so," said Sloan, old enough to be aware that sooner

or later everyone had to have their own articles of faith. Thirty-nine did for some. And a Little Red Book for others. Some people—however long they lived—got no further than a schoolboy code; others found "My Country, Right or Wrong" was as good as any. Moses or the Medes and the Persians—all Sloan knew was that very few people managed without one altogether.

"And after unisex," prophesied the other man, "we're going to get something much worse."

"Tell me," invited Sloan, short of time though he was.

"Women's lib," said the old soldier. "Sign of real decay, that is. You mark my words—women in power means the men aren't up to much. Stands to reason, doesn't it?"

"A bad sign," agreed Sloan gravely. "Civilisation on the way out and all that."

"Though," said Palfreyman in a belated attempt at fairness, "the Amazons were a well-run tribe. Many's the time I've heard Professor Teed say so. . . . I daresay you'll have heard of him, Inspector. Most people have, what with television and his books. You can see him through the glass door. Look—over there."

As it happened, as the Head Porter was speaking Professor Timothy Teed was laying down the law about something other than Amazons. The time of day made very little difference to the Professor's loquacity. Indeed, unkind spirits said that if you put him into a darkened room and turned a light in his direction he automatically went straight into his television performance.

"Any burglar that waked him up in the night with his torch," Hugh Bennett said once, "is in for a nasty shock."

"If he gets Teed's lecture on the Scottish sporran he'll go straight away," said the friend to whom he was speaking. "And leave the swag behind."

"Teed'll sell him his book, more like," Hugh Bennett had said. "After all, they say it is the definitive work."

"They also say," said the friend, who had a lively imagination, "that it has been banned in every country in the world where they've still got censorship."

"I'm not surprised."

"And that it is now required reading among the more backward tribes of the Upper Orinoco."

"Pull the other one," Hugh Bennett said amiably.

Bennett was looking across the crowded administration

block at Professor Teed now. The ground floor was—thanks to
the Head Porter, if not to the strength of their Cause—as full
now as it had been earlier in the day. As the day of the sit-in
had approached, Bennett had concentrated his propaganda
activities on the senior members of the University. He had
long ago made the discovery that, in a protest matter, one don
was worth a hundred undergraduates. Recruiting them,
though, had been a different—and delicate—matter.

True, Mr. Basil Willacy had promised Hugh Bennett his
support without demur, but he was easily flattered and only
too glad to demonstrate his alliance with the young. He was
still struggling to show he was one of the boys.

Mr. Roger Hedden, now, though still youngish and a
sociologist to boot, had told him to get lost, and Professor
Tomlin, although notably fond of reminding everyone of how
the day had gone at Guernica, had not wanted to know.
Marriage to the daughter of a Bishop had wrought great
changes in an erstwhile rebel.

A certain circumspection had prevented Bennett from
approaching some of the older members of the Combination
Room at all. No one in his right mind, for instance, would have
asked Professor Mautby. Bernard Watkinson (Modern History)
was noted for his short answers to long questions, and
somehow Miss Hilda Linaker's mind seemed always to be on
Jane Austen—and *she* had been noted for referring only *en
passant* to the Napoleonic Wars. But Professor Timothy Teed,
Head of the Department of Social Anthropology, had been a
very different matter.

Now he was in the centre—the epicentre, actually—of the
sit-in. True to form, he was dressed in plus fours and Norfolk
jacket and the largest pair of brogues seen outside a shooting
syndicate. He was improving the shining hour by teaching.

"You see my shoes, Miss Goldsworthy?" he said, thrusting a
heavily clad foot forward in front of the person sitting next to
him—an inoffensive girl called Mary Goldsworthy.

It would have been difficult for her not to have seen them
and she nodded.

"Why have these shoes got this particular set of holes in
them?"

Mary Goldsworthy, always quiet, murmured, "I don't
know."

"You should know," he said peremptorily. "You're reading
Social Anthropology, aren't you?"

"Ye—es," she stammered.

"And you come to my lectures, don't you?"

She nodded.

"You've heard me say that every single detail of human dress has significance, haven't you?"

"Yes," she said, averting her eyes from his plus fours.

"Brogues," he announced, "used to have real holes in them. Why?"

"I . . . I . . . I don't know."

"Use your imagination, girl! Before drains. When street and sewer were one and the same . . . the holes were to let the ordure through—understand?"

Mary Goldsworthy flushed and nodded.

"I thought it was to ventilate me feet," muttered an unwashed student while Professor Teed turned his attention elsewhere. There was much for him to observe.

Near the door a Moslem youth in his first year at the University of Calleshire, though well versed in the ways of the Baghdad souk, accidentally trod on the foot of a girl near him.

"May Allah bring you sons," he murmured apologetically.

The girl—a leading pro-abortionist—looked startled.

At the back of the room a male geographer and a female Arts student were rapidly furthering each other's acquaintance.

A nearby biologist gave them a poke. "This is a sit-in, remember."

The geographer waved him away. "Don't mind us. We're only pair-bonding."

*

And in a darkened police car Detective Constable Crosby was sitting beside a middle-aged woman still tense with shock and rigid with self-control. She had hardly spoken all the way back from Berebury to Luston. Crosby, who hadn't in any case known what to say, was also silent. For a wonder, his speed had been equally muted.

Now that the police car was approaching the town of Luston, though, he turned his attention from the wheel for a moment.

"Left at the bottom of the hill," she said, answering his unspoken question. "Then right and right again at the traffic lights."

He hadn't been in Miss Marion Moleyns' house more than half a minute before he was on the telephone to Sloan.

"It's chaos, sir! The whole place has been taken apart. . . ."

13
———————

Cut-over

The hawkish Dr. Kenneth Lorimer, Master of Tarsus, and the Vice-Chancellor of the University were still in conclave. The scene, though, had shifted. No longer were they sitting comfortably and over-long after dinner at the Vice-Chancellor's house with the other Heads of Colleges. Now they were back in the more workmanlike setting of the Master's room at Tarsus College. This was where Sloan ran them to ground.

"Coffee, Inspector?" John Hardiman, the Bursar, was in attendance in his usual role of universal acolyte.

"Your policewoman?" asked the Vice-Chancellor immediately. "I hope she's all right?"

"Nobody's tried to attack her so far," said Sloan.

"I am not in a position," said the academic precisely, "to know if that is good or bad for your plans, but I can certainly assure you that the other young lady . . ."

"Bridget Hellewell," said Hardiman.

". . . is quite safe and sound in our spare room. My wife," said the Vice-Chancellor, "reported that she was asleep before we left."

"Good," said Sloan warmly. There were, in fact, two policemen watching over the Vice-Chancellor's house, too, tonight, but Sloan saw no reason for acquainting him with this information.

"Inspector," said Dr. Lorimer impatiently, "what exactly is going on in this University?" The Master of Tarsus was a man who believed in taking the initiative in conversation: it almost always made for difficulty.

"Murder," responded Sloan briefly. "At least."

"At least?" Lorimer look startled.

"I can't tell you everything else yet, but there will be the reason for the murder as well, don't forget. That will have been going on, too, sir, won't it?"

"At this University? Here? But . . ." He halted. The University Grants Committee was never far from Dr. Lorimer's thoughts: murder wouldn't further his case with that Committee.

"That I can't tell you yet, sir. Not whether it was here or not. But it will emerge."

The Vice-Chancellor was a realist, too. "That's what I am afraid of."

"But here . . ." Dr. Lorimer appeared to have some difficulty in absorbing this point.

"The murder was here, Kenneth," rumbled the Vice-Chancellor, "so it's not unreasonable to postulate that its, er, *raison d'être* might be here too."

The Master of Tarsus was not the first man that Sloan had seen unsuccessfully grappling with the proximity of unpleasantness. Facts were easy enough to grasp; it was the nearness of nastiness that most people didn't like.

He cleared his throat and spoke again. "If it's any help to you gentlemen, the police have been able to rule out some of the more usual motives for the murder of a young man."

"Good," said the Vice-Chancellor with visible relief. In his day he had been a noted classical scholar, and he did not need anything spelled out. "I'm sure that's a great help."

"It narrows the field," said Sloan cautiously.

"That's something. Have you, er, anything else to tell us?"

Sloan took the cup of coffee that John Hardiman had conjured up from somewhere. "It's a little early to say but we think it might be that Moleyns had, er, so to speak—found something."

"Don't you mean found something out?" pounced Lorimer.

"Perhaps that, too," rejoined Sloan mildly.

"The Inspector," observed the Vice-Chancellor, "will no doubt have grounds for what he is saying."

Lorimer swallowed hard and adopted a slightly less inquisitorial tone. "You mean that he might have made a discovery?"

"Henry Moleyns' home in Luston was completely ransacked this evening while his aunt was over here," said Sloan, answering them both.

The Vice-Chancellor was onto the other implications of this before Dr. Lorimer had absorbed the gist of the original.

"Inspector, if someone was over in Luston tearing Moleyns' house apart, then that person couldn't have been here attacking your decoy policewoman."

"No, sir, they couldn't, could they? Not yet."

"Perhaps that's the reason why all's quiet."

"Perhaps, sir."

"The night's not over, of course."

"Not by a long chalk, it isn't," agreed Sloan.

"I hope, Inspector, that you haven't anything else on your plate just now," said Dr. Lorimer, catching up and not to be outdone.

"No more than usual, sir," said Sloan.

"I trust it's a quiet night in the town anyway." Lorimer contrived to sound patronizing even if he hadn't intended to.

Sloan suppressed an impolitic remark about the natives still being friendly and said in a rather constrained way instead that there had been a fraud case building up in one of the villages all day.

"Ah, fraud," said Lorimer. "How interesting."

"And," said Sloan quickly (before unguardedly saying something equally unwise about people who lived in glass and ivory towers not throwing stones), "one of the chemists' shops at this end of the High Street was broken into earlier this evening."

"Drugs, I suppose." All Vice-Chancellors knew all about drugs these days. It went with the job. "You two won't believe this, but when I was a young man at university the only drugs I had heard of were aspirin and morphine. Vice was confined to wine, women and tobacco."

"Then," said Sloan, his mind still on his work as a preserver of the Queen's Peace, "there's the sit-in."

The Vice-Chancellor ran a weary hand through iron-grey hair. "If anyone had told me last week, Inspector, that I could forget a sit-in here while it was still happening, I shouldn't have believed them."

"But," Sloan reminded them both, "murder takes priority."

*

It was much later when Detective Constable Crosby telephoned Sloan again. The Inspector was by then back once more in the rooms of the Tarsus don who was on sabbatical leave. Not only did the gentleman concerned have a fine taste in carpets, but unfortunately he ran to exceedingly comfortable chairs as well.

Detective Inspector Sloan had unwisely sunk into one of these when the telephone bell rang. Had he needed any confirmation that it had been a long hard day, the softly yielding way in which the cushions welcomed him would have provided it.

"Well?" he said down the line to the constable, trying to sound alert.

"Taken apart," said Crosby tersely. "The whole house. Almost."

Sloan nodded to himself and murmured, "No stone unturned."

"Drawers, cupboards, shelves—the lot," said the detective constable.

"I wonder what he was looking for?" The chair was so comfortable that Sloan was beginning to feel a certain sense of detachment stealing over him.

"Something thin and flat," said Crosby.

"How do we know that?" asked Sloan curiously.

"The carpets," said Crosby. "He had the one in Moleyns' bedroom up. And the books."

"What about them?"

"Gone through," said Crosby graphically.

"A letter?"

"Could be. He—"

"He?"

"He or she," conceded Crosby after a moment's thought. "The furniture hadn't been moved and the carpet wasn't nailed down or anything."

"He or she, then," said Sloan. For "he" you couldn't always read "she" in crime; perhaps you would be able to one day, the march of progress being what it was.

"They," said Crosby elliptically, "had the books out and on the floor."

"Something thin and flat," mused Sloan.

"I don't think we're going to know what it was, sir."

"Why not?"

"I think he—" The constable stopped and started again. "I think he or she found whatever it was they were looking for."

"What!"

"In the books."

"What books?" Sloan was quite awake now, sitting bolt upright and well away from any cushions.

"In the last book he took off the shelf, sir."

"What last book?" He mustn't shout. Not in a room like this: not down the telephone line to a constable.

"I don't know which book, sir," explained Crosby patiently. "Not exactly. I daresay I could work it out if we knew the order they were in on the shelves before."

Sloan took a deep breath. He wasn't going to sit here and have things explained to him patiently by Crosby as if he were deficient in understanding. "I wasn't," he said, controlling himself, "asking you to tell me if it was in *Alice in Wonderland* or *Peter Rabbit*, Crosby. What I want to know is, how do you know that he found it at all?"

"Because he"—the pause was so transient that it could scarcely be called reproachful—"or she stopped looking for what it was they wanted half-way along the shelf. Just like that."

"Perhaps," said Sloan with an irony that he couldn't have told was unconscious or not, "that was where you came in."

"No, sir. I didn't disturb anyone. I checked. Entry and exit were by the Yale lock on the front door. Child's play, opening them."

Sloan grunted. Love wasn't the only thing that laughed at locksmiths. "So you think he found what he was looking for?"

"In the last book," continued Crosby tenaciously.

"That was where I came in," snarled Sloan. "Remember?"

"I think that the last book, sir, was" —Sloan heard him rustle the pages of a notebook— "called *Catch-22*, by Joseph Heller."

"Was it?" Sloan ground his teeth. He must have babies on the brain. Why in the world when he came to name two books to Crosby, of all people, did a pair of children's ones come unbidden into his mind? At this rate he'd be the laughing-stock of the force long before his baby was born. With an effort he brought his mind back to the job in hand. "Anything obviously missing?"

"Miss Moleyns says not that she knows about. Mind you," qualified the constable, "she's in no real state to say. Not now. She's wandering about the house still trying to take it all in, poor woman."

"First the boy, then the house," said Sloan, glad that Crosby was at least a man of feeling. They had some men on the strength without compassion. After a while you didn't know which cases to put them on. The public, of course, thought they knew which they had.

Traffic.

"That's right," said Crosby, oblivious of this.

"Fingerprints?" asked Sloan from force of habit.

"Not so much as a smudge," said Crosby. "A real professional job."

"Just like the murder," said Sloan, unsurprised. "What in the name of goodness is a man who knows how as well as that doing at a university?"

"Aftercare?" suggested Crosby.

"They do have some dotty schemes," said Sloan grimly, "but I don't think they are as daft as that yet." The despairing part was that you could never be sure with do-gooders. Never.

"I've heard," said Crosby, "that the Russians go in for rehabilitation in a big way."

"That," retorted Sloan smartly, "only goes to show that you shouldn't believe all that you heard."

"No, sir." He coughed. "Shall I stay on here?"

"No. What I want you to do, Crosby, is to lay on someone from Luston to keep an eye on things over there—particularly Miss Moleyns—until morning and for you to make your way back here."

"To help Battling Bertha, sir?"

"It doesn't look as if she needs it."

"She never has," said Crosby.

"I wasn't thinking about her being a fine figure of a woman," said Sloan: the Amazons had certainly made their mark on the world.

"No, sir."

"It's just that no one's been near the sanatorium so far."

"Someone didn't need to worry about Moleyns' last words, then, did they, sir?"

"He'd got eyes, Crosby," said Sloan irritably. "He wasn't stabbed in the back. He must have seen who did it."

"If he did," insisted Crosby doggedly, "then he didn't know them, sir, did he, or he would have said, wouldn't he, to that girl who found him."

"Bridget Hellewell," said Sloan, following the convolutions of the sentence as best he could.

"Instead of what he did say," said Crosby.

"Did you try the words 'twenty-six minutes' on the aunt?"

"Yes, sir. They didn't mean a thing to her."

"Nor to me," said Sloan, adding obscurely, "nor to anyone
else we've asked, which by no means means that it doesn't
mean anything at all."

"No, sir."

"On the contrary," said Sloan, thinking as he said it that he
was beginning to sound like one of the dons himself. (He put
this down, quite illogically, to his sybaritic surroundings.)

"Yes, sir." Crosby cleared his throat. "Sir . . ."

"Yes?"

"There was one thing."

"It is already late," remarked Sloan, "so if you would get to
the point."

"I asked Miss Moleyns for a photograph of the deceased, like
you said."

Sloan had made it standard practice years ago. Sometimes
photographs were more than relatives could bear. They went
home from the police mortuary and tore them up. All of them.
Straight away.

"Well?" he asked.

"She went to have a look and then what with the chaos
everywhere she didn't quite know where to begin."

"So?"

"So she said that of course there would be one in his
passport and she did know where he kept that."

Sloan groaned. "Don't tell me . . ."

"It wasn't there," said Crosby.

"Was it here, then?" said Sloan. "In his room at Tarsus?"

"No," said Crosby positively. "I would have found it if it had
been there."

Sloan conceded this at once. "This place that Henry
Moleyns kept it . . ."

"Top drawer of the little desk in his room," said Crosby
promptly.

"So that, at least, would have been found straight away."

"If it was there." Crosby was beginning to argue like a
professor, too, now: taking nothing for granted.

"And it wasn't the passport that was in the book?" Had it
really been *Catch-22?*

"No. The aunt thinks the passport was in the drawer the day
after Henry Moleyns went back to University. She tidied the
room after he'd gone and put something else in the drawer.
She can't swear to it but she's almost sure she noticed the
passport then."

"He'd been somewhere, then," concluded Sloan flatly. "Crosby, do you realise that this means . . ."

The quiet of the don's room at Tarsus and the ordered business-like tenor of Detective Inspector Sloan's telephone conversation with his constable in Luston were interrupted by the alien sound of the bleep of Sloan's personal radio. He put the telephone down and turned his attention to the new speaker.

It was Police Constable Carpenter calling him up from the darkness of the bushes near the University Sanatorium.

His voice came over full of suppressed excitement.

"Someone came out of the Tarsus quadrangle, sir. About a minute ago. He kept out of the light—he took good care about that, so I can't tell you anything about him . . . then he disappeared along the edge of the building. . . . I couldn't see where he went after that . . . ah . . . oh . . ."

There was an indeterminate sound that could have been a scuffle.

"Carpenter!" snapped Sloan urgently.

There was another confused sound that could have been anything at all and then the radio went quite dead.

14

Corps-à-corps

His son would play on the wing. He was sure about that now.

At various times in the past few months Sloan had toyed with the idea that it might be in other positions on the Rugby field. After all, the halves held the team together and the centres were vital to good play and it was universally agreed that nobody could easily do without a stout-hearted full-back.

But it was as he bolted out of the room at Tarsus that was doing duty as a murder headquarters and shot down the corridor towards the College quadrangle at great speed that he finally decided that his unborn son would play as a wing three-quarter.

As he reached the quadrangle he was confronted with the

same choice that several other people had had to make before him earlier that evening: whether to cross the quadrangle diagonally in the dark, which was quicker, or to go round the two sides of the square, which were the better lit.

He hesitated there for a split second, highly conscious of all the others who had also had to choose between the same two options that day. What they had decided then had made a difference. For one thing, it had made a difference to what had been found and when.

Bridget Hellewell for one. Her choice had been to go round the quadrangle and the consequence of her making that particular choice had been the discovery of a dying man: a dying man whose last words had not been to name his murderer, a dying man whose last words had been confusing, to say the least.

Miss Hilda Linaker for another.

The don had opted for the shorter route across the quadrangle because she was not frightened of the dark, because she was as familiar with Tarsus by night as by day, because . . . because . . . because . . . He didn't really know what had prompted her selection.

Polly Mantle, too.

Polly Mantle, who seemed to be totally unconnected with anybody or anything in the situation, had entered upon the scene at that moment. Superintendent Leeyes—or rather William Shakespeare—would have underlined that with a stage direction: like "enter Ghost, armed." That had been the Superintendent's favourite in *Hamlet*. Sloan's own choice, when magnanimously offered it by the Superintendent, had been "enter two Clowns, with spades," but Polly Mantle had just appeared without benefit of playwright, so to speak. She had, apparently quite fortuitously, met up with Miss Linaker and set off with her across the quadrangle. This, the essential policeman in Sloan told him, could mean practically anything at all—or nothing.

The spin-off of the selection made by the distaff side had been the finding of the property which had been taken from Colin Ellison's room the night before, and thereby the helping to pin-point the time at which all of it had been left by the fountain. The books and papers had not been there for very long—or they would indubitably have been discovered earlier. Stephen Smithers, for instance, would have seen them as he scuttled by.

Smithers was another whose choice had made a difference. The boy with hay-fever and a face like a rabbit's had passed this way, too, at what court reporters would always insist on calling the material time. Sloan flipped back in his mind what Smithers had said in the same way that readers turn over the pages of a book looking for what they remember reading. Smithers had said that he had seen—among others—Colin Ellison as he crossed the quadrangle to the Madrigal and Glee Club meeting.

Sloan called Colin Ellison to mind without difficulty. What was more difficult about Colin Ellison was placing him in a picture which included murder. Colin Ellison, victim of temporary and apparently meaningless theft, pacifist and active non-demonstrator—if such a hybrid animal existed, clever dick (had that—could that—expression possibly be associated with the police or was he getting fanciful now?)—a habitual late-for-supper man, who, whatever he was telling them about "where he was and when," wasn't telling them the truth. Colin Ellison had been in the vicinity of the quadrangle, too, though, at about half past seven.

And did half past seven really mean twenty-six minutes past? Sloan didn't know.

Another face swam into his mind.

Henry Moleyns.

Not for one moment had Detective Inspector Sloan forgotten Henry Moleyns. The dead student, too, had exercised his option. In mid-step Sloan wondered why Moleyns had gone round and not across the quadrangle: and then the answer came to him. There hadn't been any need for a real choice on Moleyns' part, not when he came to think of it. The Chaplain's office whither he was bound was to be reached only down that side of the quadrangle if Moleyns had been approaching—and a hundred to one he had been—from the Porter's Lodge and the main part of the College. There would probably have been no need for Henry Moleyns to have decided that one at all.

And that would have made the choice of someone else quite easy.

The murderer.

Sloan hadn't forgotten the murderer, either. He was prepared to bet now that the murderer had known which way Henry Moleyns would come because he reckoned that the murderer knew all about the appointment with the Chaplain. Just as the murderer had known enough about Moleyns' attempt to see the Professor of Modern History to abstract the letter making that appointment from the student's pigeonhole. Someone hadn't wanted Moleyns to see Professor Watkinson and had no intention of letting him see the Chaplain, either.

But by letting that appointment with the Reverend C. A. T. Pollock stand, that person had known exactly which way his victim would come and almost as precisely when.

All this was no more than a few quick flashes through Sloan's mind—which was by now thoroughly awakened—as he pounded towards the quadrangle from his murder headquarters. In the event, he himself went round, not across—his son would be a winger all right—speed was the thing and the quadrangle was faintly better lit. Bridget Hellewell had been right about this—and he didn't want to end up in the fountain with the goldfish.

As he sped along the paving stones towards the far end where the quadrangle yielded to the archway that led to the grounds and then to the sanatorium beyond, Sloan felt for his torch. He had it in his hand before he decided not to switch it on. Instead he put a brake on his run and listened. Then he came out of the lighted quadrangle both cautiously and quietly.

He moved out into the night himself and waited for a moment until he could see better.

There were no flashing lights that he could see and no sounds coming from anywhere in the grounds. He glanced quickly up to the sanatorium window. There were no lights on there and no shouting or other disturbance emanating from that direction. It looked as though Battling Bertha was undisturbed—for the time being, anyway.

Once his eyes had adjusted themselves and he had orientated himself in the near-darkness, he looked towards the spot where he had last seen Constable Carpenter and started to make his way towards that. With Red Indian stealth, he put one foot in front of the other, keeping the tree that he had noticed earlier well in view. It was as he approached it that he heard a most curious sound—a sort of slapping.

He could see better now.

There was a figure supine on the ground and another figure bending over it: doing something.

Sloan changed his mind about his son being a wing three-quarter at much the same time as he launched himself in the direction of both figures. There was no doubt about it. His boy was going to be a scrum half.

"Got you!" he said, landing fairly and squarely on the upper figure of the two.

"But I didn't mean to hurt him," gasped Colin Ellison, from under the weight of a well-built Detective Inspector of Police. "Honestly!"

*

"Let me see, now," said Superintendent Leeyes heavily, "Colin Ellison is the one who claimed to be a pacifist, isn't he?"

"He is," agreed Sloan: Constable Carpenter was going to require quite a bit of convincing on that point.

The night was really getting on now but he had known that Leeyes wouldn't have gone home. Nor would he have come to the scene of the crime, of course. That sort of work he always insisted was routine and, like all routine work, best left to those used to doing it. "The greatest danger to good investigation," he would pronounce in rare moments of expansion, "is the fingerprints of top brass who are underfoot." Sloan agreed with the sentiment, however expressed, and had telephoned him at the Berebury Police Station confident that he would still be there.

"Hardly a progress report, is it, Sloan?" he remarked unhelpfully when he had heard the story through.

"He hit Carpenter," said Sloan doggedly.

"That means something," agreed Leeyes, "but what?"

"He says that he just stumbled on him in the dark, didn't know who he was or what he was doing there and hit him to be on the safe side before Carpenter had time to clobber him."

"Assaulting a police officer in the execution of his duty," intoned Leeyes.

"He said," murmured Sloan neutrally, tempering what the angry student had naturally declared with great vigour, "that he couldn't be expected to know that a man sitting under a tree on a dark night contemplating he knew not what was a police officer executing his duty or anything else."

"For a pacifist he must have packed quite a punch," observed Leeyes appreciatively. "Carpenter's a big man. Mind you, remember some of the peace lovers on some of those early nuclear protest marches. . . ."

"Carpenter can't remember what hit him," said Sloan, "but he's still cross."

Cross constables never had disturbed the Superintendent: he'd never have been promoted if they had. "And what," he asked, "does Ellison say he was doing in the College grounds at this hour of the night?"

There was always this feeling in police minds that what went on after dark as opposed to in daylight needed a second look. The law had taken note of the difference, too. . . .

"He won't say," answered Sloan. It was, in fact, the only point that the student was prepared to be silent on. "He just tells me that he doesn't have to answer any enquiries that are put to him or to make a statement if he doesn't want to or to come to the Police Station unless charged."

"That's what education does for you," said Leeyes. "I always said it was a bad thing."

Sloan wondered if he should point out that it was Judges' Rules that did that for you but decided against it.

"What about your set-up in the sanatorium?" enquired the Superintendent.

"No one's been near the place," said Sloan, still puzzled about this. "Smith and Collet and the others heard Carpenter on their radios and were on their toes waiting for the attack—"

"I remember waiting before we went ashore at Walcheren, Sloan—"

"And it didn't come," interposed Sloan swiftly. "If Ellison was meaning to get into the sanatorium, all I can say is that he didn't go ahead. He told me he just bent over Carpenter, slapping his face, and was trying to bring him round. That's when I found him."

"Would he," asked Leeyes with great pertinence, "have had time to get back to Berebury and attack Carpenter after turning over Henry Moleyns' aunt's house in Luston?"

"Yes," said Sloan unhesitatingly. "It's not all that far. You'd need transport, of course."

That was one of the things he should be getting someone to look into now: he needed to know who of all those they were concerned about had the means to get over to Luston from Berebury. Not, of course, he reminded himself, that he had had all that much time to spare since Constable Crosby had rung.

The Superintendent, needless to say, never let a little matter like practical considerations come between him and his enquiries. "And who else," he asked, "could have got there and back without being accounted for besides Colin Ellison?"

"A great many people," replied Sloan grimly. To all intents and purposes, everyone who hadn't actually been locked up by Palfreyman in the Almstone administration block since the sit-in started.

"I hear," remarked Leeyes conversationally, "that they've still got old Wheatley there."

"I know," said Sloan slowly. Nobody needed to be too imaginative to guess the sort of gibes that would come the way of the police when news of Dr. Wheatley's incarceration got known in Calleshire.

"I did think they'd ask us to get him out," said Leeyes, "but they haven't."

"Talk about law and order," muttered Sloan.

"Ah, talk about it . . . that's easy," said Leeyes sagely. "It's the doing that's difficult."

"At least we know where Dr. Wheatley is," said Sloan. "That's more than we can say for some of the others."

"Such as?"

"Professor Mautby." Sloan pulled his notebook out of his pocket with his spare hand. "He came into College to go to his laboratory just before all this blew up."

"What for?"

"He knows. I don't. He's sitting there saying he's only working and doesn't know what all the fuss is about."

Leeyes grunted. "What about the others?"

"Neil Carruthers, Roger Hedden, Tomlin and old McLeish all seem to be at home."

"'Don hypocritical, Don bad, Don furtive, Don three-quarters mad . . .' Where did I learn that, Sloan?"

"I couldn't say, sir, I'm sure." In his time the Superintendent had been to so many evening classes that you could be sure neither of what he did know nor of what he didn't.

"Professor Watkinson we're looking for now. He's Modern History. He's still not back from giving a lecture to the Calleford Historical Society."

"It's getting late."

"As he's a bachelor," said Sloan, a note of irony creeping into his voice, "no one knows if he's expected back tonight or not."

"As a married man," said Leeyes instantly, "I can tell you he's got a lot to be thankful for."

"And Peter Pringle," said Sloan, ignoring both his own wife and her condition. "He's the Librarian."

"What about him?"

"He is said to be away for the night," replied Sloan. "In Bodley."

"Is that," enquired Leeyes truculently, "the same as in Chancery?"

"In Oxford," said Sloan. "It's another library."

"Well, find out if he's still there. The Oxford police," said the Superintendent, still being difficult, "will understand. They've had a university there even longer than we have."

"Then," persisted Sloan, "there's Miss Hilda Linaker."

"Not there?"

"Not anywhere," said Sloan worriedly.

15

Hit

"Chinese take-away," announced Detective Constable Crosby, dumping a collection of small cartons down on the table belonging to the don whose room at Tarsus College they were using. It was a very beautiful oval table made of rosewood—a fact which appeared to have completely escaped the notice of the constable.

"I suppose," said Sloan meaningly, looking at his watch, "that you're waiting for me to ask what kept you."

"There's not a lot of other drivers on the road, sir, not this time of night."

"That I can well believe," said Sloan with some spirit. "When they see you coming they get off it if they can."

"Sweet and sour," announced Crosby, concentrating on opening the first package.

"Was it," enquired Sloan, still doing some calculations with time and distance, "a personal best?"

"Luston to Berebury, sir, yes." Crosby sounded satisfied. Driving fast motor cars fast was about the only aspect of his police work known to really interest the detective constable:

he was always trying to beat his own course record in the country.

"Damage?"

"Ah . . . bean shoots." Crosby appeared to be giving all his attention to the food. "Damage, sir?" he said assiduously. "What damage?"

"Suppose," said Sloan implacably, "you tell me."

"A hen. At least I think it was a hen." He opened the next carton. "Oh, good! Chicken."

If Detective Constable Crosby saw no incongruity in this, then Detective Inspector Sloan saw no point in underscoring it.

"Anything else?" he asked.

"There was a bicyclist, sir. . . ."

Sloan groaned. "Don't tell me. . . ."

"Chop suey. That's nice."

"Crosby!"

The constable squinted at him uneasily. "He might write in."

Sloan breathed out. "As long as he's alive to tell the tale."

"He looked a bit upset."

"Is that the lot? Nothing more?"

"Lychees," said Crosby, still opening packages and ignoring the carefully cherished patina of the rosewood.

"Somewhere," observed Sloan mordantly, "there is someone who loves that table."

"What table? . . . Oh, sorry." He produced a handkerchief of young bandanna proportions and colour and mopped away.

"I'm glad you had time for the shopping as well," remarked Sloan astringently. He'd just worked out Crosby's average speed: what the upper level had been he didn't dare think.

"Velly quick service," said the constable, grinning. He pushed a *mélange* of what he had brought back in Sloan's direction. "Here, sir. Try this."

It wasn't an hour at which Sloan usually ate. If he had been asked he would have declared that he wasn't hungry. To his surprise neither factor stopped him eating with relish. Buddha might have managed on a single grain of rice a day: Sloan found several hundred more satisfying. By the time he had finished eating, the world looked a slightly more promising place.

The same feeling must have overtaken the detective constable, too, because he said quite cheerfully, "Just Miss Linaker missing, sir?"

"Isn't that enough?" growled Sloan.

"Nobody else, I mean?"

"Not Professor Mautby anyway," said Sloan with feeling. "He's still over in his precious laboratory. He's been there for half the night. I've got someone watching him now—not that they can see much of what he's up to. And I daresay they'd understand less if they could see more."

"I don't suppose that there's anyone here that would understand it, sir, even if they could see," said Crosby comfortably. "They say he's very clever. Miss Moleyns told me that Henry kept on telling her that."

"Professor Watkinson," said Sloan, consulting his notebook, "finished his talk to the Calleshire Historical Society just before ten o'clock and then went off with all the men on the Committee for a drink at the Tabard in Calleford. Nobody seems to know what's happened to him since closing time."

"Ah," said the constable expressively.

"Ah, indeed," echoed Sloan.

"He could be anywhere, then."

"Mr. Peter Pringle," said Sloan, one eye still on his notebook, " is said to be spending the night with an old friend at Oxford and driving back first thing in the morning. The Library opens again tomorrow."

"Just the milkman on the road, then, if you're early enough," said Crosby knowledgeably.

"You've got a one-track mind," said Sloan—and immediately regretted it. In a university it should be the others who went in for the double meanings: not the police.

"Yes, sir." It was impossible to tell if the pun had registered.

"And Colin Ellison . . ."

" 'A Hard Day's Night,' " observed Crosby suddenly.

"What?"

"It's a song title, sir."

"What about it?"

"It's us, isn't it?"

"Crosby, are you having me on?"

"No, sir. Honest. It's the title of a song. I just thought it's us, isn't it, sir? We're having a hard day's night, aren't we?"

"If we're going in for titles," said Sloan grimly, "*Crime and Punishment* has a lot to be said for it. Now, where was I?"

Constable Crosby wasn't exactly making the hard day's night

any easier himself but Sloan saw no point in going into that. . . .

"Colin Ellison, sir."

"Master Colin Ellison," said Sloan with determination, "whether he likes it or not, is spending the rest of the night under lock and key at the Police Station."

"So he's accounted for," said Crosby.

"Everyone else," said Sloan, suddenly weary, "is either at the sit-in or in their own beds because we've checked, but without exception they could all have got over to Luston before you did."

"And one of 'em's a murderer. Lychees, sir?"

*

The two policemen were interrupted by the jangling of the telephone bell.

"Your call's through, sir," said Crosby, handing over the receiver, "to something that sounds like Petty France. Can that be right?"

It was a strange place-name for the office of Her Britannic Majesty's Passport Office. Sloan would have been the first to admit that. After a moment or two on the telephone he was also, to his surprise, prepared to admit something else.

That our civil servants are wonderful, too.

In their own way, that is.

The young man on night duty in the Passport Office sounded alert and co-operative. "Not a simple loss, I take it, Inspector?"

"Stolen, we think," said Sloan, "from a house in Luston, Calleshire, earlier this evening. There are, er, other troubles."

"Ah, I see. Well, our first concern would be that no one uses it to leave the country with—"

"Naturally."

"If you will excuse me for a moment. . . ."

Sloan hung on. The young man, too, had his priorities. He must have had his accustomed routines as well, because he didn't keep Sloan waiting long.

"Now, Inspector . . ."

"We'd like to know when it was issued," said Sloan.

"Two years ago last July."

That figured. Henry Moleyns' first trip abroad had been with his school. For tasters.

"And to check that it hasn't been handed in or reported as lost," said Sloan. He was too old a hunter to be caught chasing wild geese.

"Moleyns, Henry Arthur . . ." The young man seemed to be consulting some sort of card index. "No, Inspector, we do not appear to have any note of that happening."

"It was never likely, I agree," said Sloan. "He only got back home on Monday from his bicycle trip round Europe and he would have needed it then."

"Our water guard would have seen to that," said the young man quaintly.

"This passport," said Sloan, firmly ignoring the archaism, "tell me how far he could have gone with it."

"Any country in the world," said the civil servant promptly, "except those requiring a visa as well."

Definitely not the same, thought Sloan to himself, as going where the 'ell you liked.

"Where would he need a visa for?" he asked curiously.

The voice in Petty France drew breath. "The Iron Curtain countries . . . the Bamboo curtain countries . . ."

It was very nearly, decided Sloan, the same as the lights going out all over Europe, this coming down of curtains around continents.

"The Middle East . . ."

Sloan didn't blame them there. A perpetual tinderbox; the only wonder, that there was not more trouble in the Middle East than there was.

"Most South American countries . . ."

It was their exit facilities that usually interested the police more than their entrance ones. The small print of extradition treaties was equally closely studied by both the criminal fraternity and New Scotland Yard's legal department.

"The United States of America . . ."

"This visa," said Sloan. ("Give me your tired, your poor . . .") "Tell me what it looks like."

"It's usually a full-page stamp on the passport."

"Done by?"

"The Consular Office of the country which the passport holder proposes to visit."

"And that office," said Sloan slowly, thinking hard, "would therefore be the only place which would know whether such a visa had been issued?"

"That is so," said the young man.

"And without the passport we wouldn't know?" That was saying the same thing in different words.

"If by 'we' you mean the United Kingdom government . . ."

"I do." He didn't always, but he did now.

"Then that is so."

*

Never a man to stand on ceremony, Crosby had finished the lychees.

"Moleyns had been somewhere," announced Sloan, putting down the telephone, "and my guess is that it showed on his passport."

"So no passport," concluded Crosby simplistically.

"No passport," said Sloan, "which proves that someone didn't want anyone to know where he'd been."

"Even after he was dead," remarked Crosby, licking a stray splash of lychee juice from his finger.

"My guess is that he went somewhere you need a visa for," said Sloan. He looked round the room. "Do you suppose the comfort-lover that lives here possesses anything as ordinary as an atlas?"

They eventually found one on the bookshelves. Crosby laid it on the rosewood table. "Where do you want to look?"

"North-west Europe. We think that Moleyns got as far as Cologne."

"Cologne." The constable turned up the index. "'See Köln.'"

"Then do that thing."

Crosby dived into the index again. "Page 48, M 48 + 509."

"Latitude and longitude," said Sloan, putting his finger on Cologne without difficulty. "That's where Miss Moleyns had his postcard from. . . . Wherever he went, I reckon he brought something back with him."

"Something flat and thin," supplied Crosby.

"Something that would fit in a book."

"*Catch-22*," said the constable.

"The book is immaterial," declared Sloan as grandly as Lady Bracknell ever did.

"Yes, sir."

"Something that could be used as evidence of where he'd

been," continued Sloan, working it out as he went along, "or of what he'd found when he got there."

"That he didn't want anyone else to know about," supplemented Crosby.

"Otherwise he wouldn't have hidden it," agreed Sloan.

"Blackmail?" said Crosby.

"Blackmailers don't usually make appointments with the Chaplain," said Sloan, "but there's always the first time."

"Somebody was ready to tear the place apart, sir. You should have seen Miss Moleyns' house."

"So it was important," mused Sloan. "I don't think we need be in any doubt about that."

"More important than Henry Moleyns' life," said Crosby trenchantly, "because he got killed for it."

"He got killed before he could tell the Chaplain, remember." Sloan was still pursuing his own train of thought.

"Before he could tell anyone," came Crosby's antiphon.

"He tried, though," said Sloan, his mind going back to the darkened quadrangle and the girl Bridget Hellewell. "Didn't he?"

"But 'twenty-six minutes' was as far as he got." Crosby tidied up the remnants of their impromptu meal and said prosaically, "It's not a lot to go on, sir, is it?"

"What I think we had better do next," said his superior, "is to concentrate on finding the Professor of English Literature."

*

It was quite possible that out of all those of and having business to do with the University of Calleshire only Matron, serene in her calling and secure in her sanatorium, slept really well that night. Certainly the slumbers of Dr. Herbert Wheatley were very nearly as troubled as those of Shakespeare's King Richard the Third the night before the Battle of Bosworth Field.

True, Dr. Wheatley was not visited by visions of the avenging, but his sleep was still an uneasy one. In the first place, the administrator's chair was no substitute for his own interior-sprung mattress, and in the second, the Almstone administration block did not compare with his own bedroom for peace and quiet.

As the night wore on, the noises off died down and even the more frenetic students sought some sleep. It was quite another sensation that then came between Dr. Wheatley and perfect repose.

It was one quite unfamiliar to the good doctor.

Hunger.

In this he differed from the undergraduates. Apparently sustained by a mixture of excitement and coffee, they ate little during their occupation: and were in any case used to eating as and when they could catch a meal. Dr. Wheatley's digestive system was accustomed to both regular work and the soporific nightly bonus of the College port (laid down—with an eye to the future—by Professor McLeish when declared vintage). Without either sustenance or quietening mixture, the Dean's digestive juices sent signals of distress to their owner throughout the night.

Another source of disquietude had been Malcolm Humbert.

Malcolm Humbert, sometime student, had come through from the sit-in to have a chat with him. It was many years since Dr. Wheatley had enjoyed talking to any man after one o'clock in the morning: and never to the Malcolm Humberts of this world. "Talking" was perhaps an exaggeration. Humbert spoke and Dr. Wheatley listened—for a time, anyway. Then, with a technique perfected over the years at tutorials and committees, he stopped listening.

It was the nearest that he came to real sleep that night.

*

Dawn on the Friday morning was observed by more people than those who usually took note of it. For one of them it was to be the last dawn that person was going to see.

The policemen on guard in the grounds round the sanatorium saw it first, shook themselves stiffly and thought about bacon and eggs in their canteen. The Vice-Chancellor saw it from his bedroom window and thought about newspaper reporters. Colin Ellison saw it through his cell window in Berebury Police Station ("that little tent of blue Which prisoners call the sky") and thought about what he was going to say to someone later that day.

Dr. Herbert Wheatley became aware of it in the Almstone administration block and thought wistfully of the packet of antacid tablets in his dressing-gown pocket in his bedroom at home. It was seen by Peter Pringle, College Librarian and Keeper of Books, rising early in Oxford and breakfasting en route as he drove back to Berebury and the Greatorex Library. Detective Inspector Sloan saw it from his murder headquarters in Tarsus College and thought about Miss Hilda Linaker, who had returned to her rooms from heaven only knew where half-way through the night, insisting that she hadn't been able to sleep and so had gone for a walk.

Detective Constable Crosby saw the dawn, too, and considered—not for the first time—his nocturnal encounter with Professor Bernard Watkinson. In its way it had been memorable—but not for its clarity. Professor Watkinson had returned to Tarsus College from Calleford in a highly ebullient mood. The ebullience, however, had turned to belligerence when he was asked to account for his movements after dinner.

He could, it transpired, have driven without difficulty to the Moleyns home in Luston before going on to Calleford to deliver his lecture.

"On Clausewitz, Constable. Ever heard of him?"

"Can't say that I have, sir, unless he's one of those gypsies down by the river. They've got funny names and there's one with a turn in his eye—"

"Clausewitz was a Prussian soldier."

"Then I haven't," said Crosby firmly.

"He wrote on the nature of war," said Watkinson a little thickly.

"Did he, sir?"

"He said you needed two people to make war." The Professor seemed to have some trifling difficulty adjusting his glasses.

Crosby had considered what he said. "Then I reckon he might be right, sir. It's not war if one side won't fight, is it, sir? It's something else."

"True, O wise young constable."

"Yes, sir," said Constable Crosby stolidly. "Now, sir, if I might just trouble you for the names and addresses of the gentlemen you spent the rest of the evening with in the Tabard—it was the Tabard, wasn't it, sir?—in Calleford—"

"War is never an isolated act." An owlish look had come over the Professor of Modern History.

"No, sir, I'm sure it isn't."

"The result in war is never absolute. Clausewitz said that too."

"What about sitting down and having a little rest, sir?"

"'The political object reappears afterwards.'"

"Very likely, sir. Try this chair, sir. . . . No, not that way, sir. . . . That's a cupboard. . . ."

Professor Simon Mautby saw the dawn from his study window as he marked the last of the vacation studies handed in by the second-year ecology students. It was one of his cardinal principles that each day's work was done before the next day's work was started. He put his red pencil through something Polly Mantle had written about a Lombardy poplar ("Just because she was in Italy . . .") and scribbled "Leave out the bosky, boy" in the margin of the last essay. Then he piled the papers up ready to leave at the Porter's Lodge on his way in to Tarsus College.

All except one, that is.

The contribution from Henry Moleyns, deceased, he put on one side in his study.

Miss Hilda Linaker still had not slept. She saw the dawn from her rooms in Tarsus, made herself a pot of tea, dressed, gathered up her academic gown and went out. There was one person whom she wanted to see very badly before her teaching day began: Peter Pringle, Librarian.

She saw him all right, but by then he was dead.

16

Derobement

Quite dead.

Everyone said so.

In the context of Mr. Peter Pringle's death "everyone" turned out to mean Miss Hilda Linaker herself, who had been the one to discover the body of the tubby little Librarian in his room, the library assistant who had come when she called out and three assorted university readers who had been working in the Library early.

Detective Inspector Sloan confirmed the fact of death as far as he could officially without a medical expert. He wasn't in a lot of doubt. The Librarian was slumped over his desk like a rag-doll, the back of his skull stove in. The murder weapon—

unconfirmed, of course—was not far away and had not been hard to find.

Sloan regarded the blood-stained bust of Jacob Greatorex, sometime benefactor of the University of Calleshire, as dispassionately as he was able.

Meanwhile the library assistant emerged as a twitterer. "Oh dear, oh dear . . ."

"I thought it was all a joke," said Stephen Smithers, who turned out to be one of the early readers. "That's why I didn't take a lot of notice."

"I saw him," Miss Linaker was saying dully. "Afterwards. Going down the corridor. Away from me. He was running, of course, but I thought that was because—"

"So did I!" exclaimed Professor Tomlin censoriously. "Naturally. It's disgraceful!"

The third of the early readers in the library was a girl who looked embarrassed. "That's why I thought it must be someone from another university. They do come for the bust, you know, quite often."

"I thought someone must have some money on it," said Smithers, who looked as if he was about to start sneezing again. "You've got to have a reason for going round like that on a cold day."

"You mean," said Sloan, somewhat at sea, "that none of you recognised whoever it was who did this?"

The girl reader flushed. "I don't know if I knew him or not, Inspector. . . . You see . . ."

"He hadn't any clothes on," said Miss Linaker abruptly.

"A streaker, you mean?" exclaimed the twitterer, excited and alarmed in turn. "I was working over by the catalogue so I didn't see—"

"Not a stitch," declared Professor Tomlin, already beginning to consider how he could best present the fact to his wife. He decided that the happiest approach might be through the Old Testament—that often went down well with Mrs. Tomlin, Bishop's daughter. . . . Some reference to Adam, say . . . the old Adam, perhaps . . . no, perhaps not. Her enquiries struck terror every bit as much as Mrs. Proudie's "Bishop, a word with you. . . ."

"The best disguise of all," said Miss Linaker bitterly. "The Emperor's clothes. . . ."

The woman don seemed to have suffered a sea-change. She had groped her way to a chair and was sitting now with her elbows on the nearest table, her head sunk into her hands. She looked suddenly a lot older.

"No clothes at all?" said the library assistant, just to be quite sure she had got it right.

"Actually," said Stephen Smithers with a certain diffidence, "I think he was wearing a stocking."

Sloan gave him a baleful look.

"Over his head," said Smithers hastily.

Sloan nodded. That, at least, made sense. So presumably, would someone's killing of Peter Pringle—unless what they were up against was a psychopath, someone who killed for the lust of killing like a fox decimating a chicken run. Somehow Sloan didn't think they were.

"But why?" demanded Professor Tomlin. "First Henry Moleyns, now poor Pringle here."

"I think," managed Miss Hilda Linaker painfully, "I may be able to tell you why."

*

"Well, why?" demanded Superintendent Leeyes truculently.

Detective Inspector Sloan had gone back to the room in Tarsus that he was using as a murder headquarters and picked up the telephone. He'd left Crosby in charge at the Greatorex Library and called over the constables who had spent the night watching the sanatorium to give him a hand. There was much to be done. Battling Bertha he'd detailed to keep an eye on Miss Hilda Linaker. The policewoman had had one of the quietest nights of all, lying guarded in the sanatorium against a danger which did not come.

That fact was something he would have to consider presently: the danger, alas, had been elsewhere.

In the meantime he was concentrating on Peter Pringle's death.

"Well," demanded Leeyes, who hadn't taken at all kindly to the news of another murder, "why?"

Sloan cleared his throat and began tentatively, "There was an old scholar of Tarsus . . ."

He stopped, aware of undertones.

"This," said Leeyes coldly, "is no time for limericks."

"No, sir." He started again. "Yesterday evening Miss Linaker had a note from the Librarian saying that he had found an

important letter among a whole load of books and papers left to
Tarsus College by a former undergraduate."

"How important?" asked Leeyes. Nobody could complain
that the Superintendent couldn't grasp essentials.

"Valuable, anyway," said Sloan. The Professor of English
Literature hadn't been able even to begin to tell him what the
letter would be worth on the open market.

Leeyes grunted. "Murder valuable, would you say?"

"I don't know, sir." There was so much he didn't know
now. . . .

"This letter," said Leeyes, still sticking to essentials.

"Yes?"

"What made it so valuable?"

"According to Pringle's note it was from Richard Wordsworth—he was a lawyer in London, it seems, and these letters
that were left to Tarsus were mostly legal ones—Algernon
Harring—he was the man who willed them to Tarsus—had
read law—"

"The letter," said Leeyes impatiently.

"From Richard Wordsworth to his brother William."

"The poet?"

"Yes."

"Letters to poets don't count for much," said Leeyes
immediately. "Letters from them might."

"This letter was different," said Sloan. He wasn't in any
doubt about that. Miss Linaker's eyes had glowed when she
had told him about it.

"What was different about it, then?"

"It named Jane Austen's lost lover," said Sloan impressively.

"Who?"

"The man Jane Austen loved." Miss Linaker's voice had
been almost reverent when she explained that there was a
growing school of thought that identified the nameless man as
John Wordsworth, another brother of William, lost at sea.

"Apparently," went on Sloan uneasily, "she wrote about a
Captain Wentworth in one of her books—*Persuasion*."

"For Wentworth read Wordsworth, you mean?"

"Something like that, sir."

"I get you," said Leeyes unexpectedly. "There was a sonnet
that Shakespeare dedicated to a Mr. W.H. that our tutor told
us about. People have been trying to place him, too, for
years."

"It looked as if this letter might prove the link between

Wentworth and Wordsworth," said Sloan, ignoring the tempting by-paths of other literary detection. "To be truthful, sir, I couldn't quite put together all that Miss Linaker was saying. She's pretty shocked finding Pringle like that—and," he added, always the policeman, "excited, too."

"This letter," said Leeyes tenaciously, "where is it now?"

"We don't know, sir. That's the trouble. All Pringle said in his note to Miss Linaker was that he'd found it."

"Moleyns," said Leeyes. "Did he know about it?"

"I don't rightly know, sir. The note to Miss Linaker was in her pigeon-hole in the Porter's Lodge. I reckon anyone could have read it."

"Have you got it?" said Leeyes, "this note from Pringle?"

"Yes."

"That's something."

"Not as much as you might think, sir."

"Oh?"

"It's typewritten, for a start," said Sloan.

"Signed?"

"Initials, that's all."

Leeyes sighed. "And this man who Miss Linaker saw running away?"

"Male and adult, sir. She can't tell us anything more than that."

"That was what she said?"

"More or less," replied Sloan, the Professor of English Literature's actual words still ringing in his ears: a quotation . . . Shakespeare, she said . . . from *A Midsummer Night's Dream*. . . .

"A proper man, as one shall see in a summer's day . . ."

*

Somehow, somewhere, sometime, Alfred Palfreyman had contrived to shave. The injustice of this bit deep into Sloan's consciousness. It was quite illogical that he should feel so disadvantaged by an eighth of an inch of stubble thrusting its way through a police chin when it had been neatly removed from an army one. And as is the way with stigmata, he couldn't keep his fingers away from it.

"It's been a rough night," observed the Head Porter, rubbing salt into the wound.

"Another death," said Sloan. That spelt failure in a murder case if anything did.

"Mr. Pringle," said Palfreyman, who had the sergeant-major's way of being well informed at all times. "By a streaker, I hear."

"Stripped to the willow," agreed Sloan.

"Clever," said Palfreyman appreciatively. "To get down to the buff, I mean."

"That's the whole trouble here," said Sloan. "Cleverness."

Palfreyman did not deny it. "And nobody saw anything, I suppose."

"I have discovered," said Sloan dryly, "that the great thing about working in a library is the Bingo approach."

"You have the advantage of me there, Inspector."

"Eyes down."

"Ah, yes." The Head Porter grinned. "And no one looked at your chap twice."

"If they did," said Sloan, "they aren't saying."

"Especially the ladies, I take it," said Palfreyman slyly.

"Especially the ladies."

"What I have noticed, Inspector," Palfreyman informed him judiciously, "about the ladies here . . ."

"Yes?"

"Is that those who have had a classical education understand pretty nearly everything that goes on."

"That I can well believe."

"And those that have studied history." He sniffed. "You can't tell them a lot, either."

"It's all happened before," agreed Sloan wearily. That would be no consolation to Miss Marion Moleyns or Mrs. Peter Pringle, of course.

"Now, the mathematicians . . ." Palfreyman drew breath. "There's one of them that doesn't know Tuesday from Christmas."

"What about Professors of Social Anthropology?" asked Sloan. "Seeing as how we're over here."

The Head Porter jerked his shoulder in the direction of the administration block and said scornfully, "Him? All our Mr. Teed really knows is which side his bread's buttered on."

"None of them could have got out and done for Mr. Pringle, could they? That's what I've really come across to check on."

Palfreyman patted his pocket and some keys clinked. "Take it from me, Inspector, they didn't. You'll have to look somewhere else for your killer. Believe you me, and like it or not, this little lot are in the clear."

*

Miss Linaker might look suddenly haggard and and concerned but she was still functioning as a thinking human being.

"Who all knew about the Harring letters, Inspector?" She frowned before she answered him. "Let me see, now . . . everyone who was at dinner on Tuesday evening, anyway. That's when Peter Pringle first told us about them. . . . Poor Peter. . . ."

"What did he say?" asked Sloan persuasively. Lamentations would have to wait upon proper investigation.

"He was complaining about the quantity, actually—sixty-seven cases of books and three of letters." She smiled wanly. "He wouldn't have complained if he'd known what was in them."

"So he didn't mention Jane Austen on Tuesday evening at all?"

She gave him a pitying smile. "Inspector, can't you see that I'd have been over at the Library like a shot if he had. Besides, I'm sure he would have told me first—before anyone else, I mean. A great discovery like this would have to be authenticated before it could be announced to the world."

"Quite so, miss." He'd finally settled for calling the Professor of English Literature "miss" for reasons that he would have been hard put to it to put into words. Matron, now, that plump, amiable, compliant woman, he'd happily called "madam" without a moment's hesitation.

"There's another thing, too, Inspector." Once started talking, Miss Linaker was finding it hard to stop. "Peter Pringle could hardly have had time to find the letter by Tuesday evening. He'd only just got back to Berebury after the vacation, too, you know."

Sloan did know.

He had a report in his file now which told him where everyone had been in their summer break from the University of Calleshire and exactly when they had got back. Professor Timothy Teed had flown to the United States of America to appear on their television (he had worn spats); Bernard Watkinson, Modern History specialist, had led a party of young men over the First World War battlefields in northern

France; the Chaplain ditto to the Holy Land (each to his own . . .). Professor Tomlin had spent some time at the home of his brother-in-law the Dean of Calleford (the Church of England's word for promotion—preferment—was an accurate one). Miss Linaker herself had gone peak-bagging in Switzerland. (Nobody, Sloan reminded himself, had actually seen the streaker carry the bust into the Librarian's room: all that anyone had seen was a man running away. That, too, needed thinking about, but not now.) Professor Simon Mautby and Roger Franklyn Hedden had both stayed on at the University through the summer; Hugh Bennett had attended a left-wing summer school; Michael Challoner had been to Czechoslovakia on a youth exchange visit for unspecified "but purely cultural" purposes; Basil Willacy had taken his mother to Torquay; Peter Pringle and his wife and children had gone walking in Scotland. . . . In fact, Detective Inspector Sloan now knew where everyone had been—except Henry Moleyns.

"So, miss, the first you knew about this famous letter was . . ."

"Thursday. Yesterday." A cloud came over her face. "Yesterday was Thursday, wasn't it?"

An aching tiredness in Sloan's bones confirmed that night had separated Thursday from Friday. He nodded.

"The first I knew about it was a note in my pigeon-hole," said the Professor, "yesterday. I went round to the Library straight away but of course it was all shut up."

"Because of the sit-in," said Sloan. He didn't know yet if the student protest had anything to do with two deaths on the campus. Some people—the press, too—would be bound to link them. There was so much he didn't know: why there was someone at the University of Calleshire who could kill so expertly . . . somewhere at the back of his mind was the conviction that if he knew the answer to that a lot of other things would fall into place.

"And Peter wasn't there either," she said.

"He'd gone to Oxford."

"So I was told," she said, "but he was expected back first thing Friday morning. For when the Library opened."

"Last night, miss. You went missing on us."

She ran a hand through her hair. "I couldn't sleep, Inspector. This letter—you don't understand how important it is—the whole literary world would be interested—the name of the man Jane Austen loved is one of the last secrets of English literature—she wasn't one of those barren sisters chanting faint hymns to the cold fruitless moon, you know."

"No, miss."

The don straightened her gown. "She couldn't have written like that if she had been."

"You need something to set you alight, miss, don't you?"

She gave him a long, straight look. "You're very perceptive for a policeman."

"We see as much life and death as the next man, miss. More, probably."

She shivered. "More good and evil, too. That's what it's all about, isn't it? Your work and mine. Good and evil—and love. That's all literature is. I don't know where the love comes in with your work."

"About half-way between the good and the evil, miss."

"Yes." She stared at him. "There's a bit of both about it, isn't there?"

"This letter, miss . . ."

She might not have been listening. "My book will have to be rewritten, of course"—a slightly fanatical note had crept into her voice—"but that's no trouble. You may not quite appreciate the significance of the letter, Inspector, but the world—my world—will."

Sloan cast his mind back without difficulty to the dead Librarian, the ebullient, perennially cheerful Peter Pringle lying dreadfully dead over his desk, and said in carefully neutral tones that he thought he did understand.

"So did someone else," said Miss Linaker quietly.

"Perhaps, miss."

She stared at him. "What do you mean?"

"This note that you said you'd had from Mr. Pringle," he said.

"Yes?"

"Could anyone have read it?"

"It wasn't sealed. Just folded over."

"How long had it been in your pigeon-hole?"

"I don't know. Higgins didn't see it being left there."

"When did you last collect your post?"

"In the morning. After breakfast."

"Which morning?"

"Yesterday, of course."

"Thursday."

"Yes."

"And it wasn't there then?"

"No. I told you I didn't find it until the evening."

"Yesterday evening."

"Yes! Higgins saw me collect it. Ask him."

"And then what did you do?"

"I went round to Peter Pringle's house in case he was back from Oxford but he wasn't expected home until first thing today."

"So?"

"So I went straight there this morning as soon as the Library opened. You don't seem to understand how important this Wordsworth letter is."

"There's just one thing that doesn't tie up, miss," said Sloan formally.

"What's that?" Her head came up with a jerk. "I do assure you, Inspector, that any letter about Jane Austen's lost lover is—"

"I'm not talking about the letter, miss."

"No? Then what—"

"I'm talking about the note from Mr. Pringle to you."

"What about it?"

"But he couldn't very well have left it in the Porter's Lodge at Tarsus for you on Thursday, could he? He left Berebury on Wednesday evening after the Library closed. He was in Oxford all day Thursday. At the Bodleian."

17

Reprise forward

Nothing added up. He would have to send for the lady mathematician at the University about whom Palfreyman had told him, the one who didn't know Tuesday from Christmas. She might not know which day of the week it was: perhaps, all the same, she could put two and two together better than he, Detective Inspector C. D. Sloan, could.

He made his way back through the quadrangle to the only place in Tarsus College which he could call, however temporarily, his own. He found Detective Constable Crosby already there waiting for him.

"It is just as well," observed Crosby with a certain melancholy, "that the chap who lives here is away for a whole year. At this rate we'll be needing it until the night before he gets back."

"I thought you were in charge at the Library."

"Reinforcements have arrived."

"I see." Sloan could also see that they could do without Crosby over there, and if they could, they did. . . .

"Dr. Dabbe's in the Library now, sir, deciding that the hole in Pringle's head could just possibly have been made by something of the size and weight of the bust of Jacob Greatorex—"

"Dr. Dabbe was giving evidence in open court, Crosby, while you were still in short trousers."

"—and probably was made by the bust of the said Jacob Greatorex, seeing how it's got Pringle's blood on it."

"Carefully cross-matched," Sloan reminded him. "Forensic pathologists don't take chances."

"You're telling me," said Crosby with audible scorn. "Do you know what he's done about the time of death?"

"No." Actually Sloan didn't care, either. His concerns were elsewhere. He wanted to know who had killed Pringle and why: not where and when and how. . . .

"He just asked when he was last seen alive and then he asked when the birthday-suit boy had been spotted."

"Well?" Two from four left two just as logically as two plus two made four: Sloan didn't suppose Alfred Palfreyman's lady mathematician would need telling that either.

"Then," declared Crosby, "he said that death had probably taken place within those two limits! How do you like that?"

"Bully for him," said Sloan sourly. "You aren't going to catch our friendly neighbourhood pathologist putting his head into a noose."

"Doctors, huh!"

"They're a cautious lot," agreed Sloan more cheerfully.

"You can't beat them for it," growled Crosby.

Sloan didn't want to beat them for it. And there was one doctor in particular—an obstetrician—who had better not take any risks at all when the time came. . . . He would telephone Margaret, his wife, presently . . . but not from any old murder headquarters . . . and not with Crosby around, either.

"Do you know, sir," the constable was saying, "what my doctor said when I had this rash on my . . ."

Crosby's medical scars would have to be dealt with in the same Draconian way as the Superintendent's battle ones.

"What I want to know most of all," said Sloan, firmly changing the subject, "is why there should happen to be a specialist in murder at this University." Even as he said it, it came to him that someone else had reminded him that they were "all specialists here." "Why? Tell me that."

"Something going on? By the way, sir, Colin Ellison doesn't like it in the cells."

"There would be something wrong with them if he did," said Sloan warmly. It was one of the things, the many things, that reformers tended to forget.

"He's asking for his Member of Parliament."

"That makes a change," remarked Sloan. "It's usually their solicitors that they want to see."

"Yes, sir. He says he's got something to tell his Member, though. Something important."

"Do you happen to know," enquired Sloan astringently, "if Ellison doesn't like it down there enough to be ready to tell us now exactly what he was up to?"

"No, sir, though whatever Ellison did, he didn't kill Mr. Pringle. He was under lock and key at the time. That's what I was checking."

"He clobbered P. C. Carpenter, though," said Sloan roundly, "and it all started with his things being stolen, remember?"

"But nothing taken," responded Crosby speedily. "He swore that it was all there when Miss Linaker and Polly Mantle found it."

"Miss Linaker . . ." She was another factor in the equation he was trying to solve. "Crosby, Colin Ellison wouldn't tell us if there had been a valuable letter there that wasn't there anymore, would he, now?"

"No, sir."

"Not if it wasn't his and shouldn't have been there in the first place anyway," said Sloan. "Any more than whoever went hunting for something in Henry Moleyns' room is going to tell us about it."

"No, sir. Sir . . ."

"Well?"

"We think it must have been Moleyns that broke into Ellison's room." He waved a report in front of Sloan. "Those ears of wheat are the same sort as each other and we've found some more in Moleyns' room here and in his bedroom at home. . . . Careless blighter. It's not proof, of course."

"Just a straw in the wind," Sloan heard himself saying. That was the worst of universities—they made you think wit a substitute for wisdom.

"Moleyns took size eight and a half shoes," carried on Crosby imperviously, "and that was the size of the footmark in Ellison's room."

"Moleyns took something," said Sloan.

"But we don't know what," pointed out Crosby.

"From Ellison's room," said Sloan.

"On Wednesday."

"Though he may have put it back again."

"Yes, sir."

"And later on, somebody—"

"But we don't know who." It was like a descant.

"Took something."

"But we don't know what." Or a dirge.

"From Moleyns' room."

"And somebody," continued Crosby in the same pessimistic vein, "has taken an old letter which everyone says is valuable from Mr. Pringle's room in the Library, if"—here he added his own rider—"that's where it was to start with."

*

Sloan was saying much the same thing a little while later to the Vice-Chancellor of the University.

Holders of high office the world over are no more immune to human feeling than the next man (however much they may encourage the illusion that they are) and the Vice-Chancellor was visibly shaken by Peter Pringle's murder. He liked his violence on the small screen: "The Pink Panther" was never like this.

"A madman, Inspector," he said, grave and concerned and totally at a loss. "We must have a madman here."

"Even that would be something," muttered Dr. Kenneth Lorimer. The Master of Tarsus, a notable warrior in committee, liked his tigers to be of the paper variety.

"We can't find this letter, gentlemen," said Sloan, punctiliously sticking to the practicalities, "anywhere."

"It would be of incalculable value, Inspector," said the Vice-Chancellor equally practically.

"And a great gain to the literary world," murmured Lorimer. He was quoted a great deal in minutes and the fact had affected his spoken prose style.

That, at least, thought Sloan, making a note, tied in with what Miss Linaker had told him.

"The world of letters," carried on the Vice-Chancellor fluently, "has always cherished the hope that one day the name of Jane Austen's lost lover would be known."

"A well-known literary mystery, was it, sir?" asked Sloan. His world had unsolved mysteries too. The Wallace case, for instance: a proper policeman's puzzle that was.

"Bless my soul, yes. Books have been written. . . ."

And men have died, said Sloan: but not aloud; and worms have eaten them.

"Rudyard Kipling wrote a poem about it"—for a moment the Vice-Chancellor put Henry Moleyns and Peter Pringle out of his mind—"and every biographer that ever was has speculated about him."

"Really, sir?"

"She was very reserved, you see, Inspector," explained Lorimer.

"Times were different then," said the Vice-Chancellor wistfully. Only the other day someone had drawn his attention to the man-hours spent in student counselling at the university.

"Nameless and dateless," said the Master of Tarsus, "that's what was said about the affair. She didn't want sympathy or anything."

"No, sir." Sloan could understand that. If anything were to happen to his Margaret . . .

"I wonder how Evelyn Pringle feels," said Lorimer uneasily, recognising that there would be no committee to help him there.

"This letter," persisted Sloan.

"The world of scholarship," said Lorimer, "would expect to see it properly enshrined in its rightful place."

"And where would that be, sir?" asked Sloan, interested in spite of himself.

"A university library. Our university library."

"There may have been someone," said the Vice-Chancellor realistically, "not quite so, er, public-spirited."

"Private gain rearing its ugly head, you mean?" responded Lorimer. That, at least, never happened on his committees.

"We get quite a lot of that in our line of country," said Sloan mildly. He wouldn't like to have to say if the police met that sentiment more often than any other, but it was certainly around much of the time.

"This letter, Inspector," said the Vice-Chancellor. "It must be somewhere. . . ."

*

"It's not at Mr. Pringle's house, sir, either," Detective Inspector Sloan was saying a little later down the telephone to Superintendent Leeyes at the Police Station. He didn't know whether the Superintendent had shaved—whether, indeed, he had been home during the night or not—and he certainly wasn't the sort of man you could ask.

Leeyes grunted.

"I've had a couple of men start to go over it," said Sloan. "Mind you, they've not had much time yet."

"The widow?"

"Mrs. Pringle?" There had been a suddenness about her transformation from wife to widow that Sloan, let alone Evelyn Pringle, needed time to assimilate. "She's gone to her sister's and taken the children with her." It came into his tired mind that these households where murder had struck were not unlike the violated birds'-nests you came across sometimes in a thicket—empty and cold, deserted after disaster, traces of predators all around. . . .

"Your friend," said the Superintendent with heavy irony, "that we're giving hospitality to . . ."

"Colin Ellison? What about him?" Sloan had almost lost interest in the student since he'd seen the Librarian lying dead across the desk while Ellison was known to be out of harm's way in a prison cell.

"He insists he wasn't on his way to clobber Bridget Hellewell in the sanatorium. Says he didn't even know she was there."

"Everyone knew she was there—or thought they did," said Sloan mechanically. "We put the word around at dinner last night."

"He says," said Leeyes with fine impartiality, "that he was late for dinner last night. And he keeps on saying he didn't know about Moleyns' even being dead until then, let alone the fine detail."

"Yes," admitted Sloan, "he was late actually. I remember being told." He'd got that down in a notebook somewhere—as he'd got everything else that everyone had said and done written down in a notebook somewhere. He said very slowly, a little bell beginning to tinkle in his mind, "Ellison had been late for dinner each evening that week, as I remember."

"Up to something," said Leeyes promptly.

"I daresay," agreed Sloan, though it was changes in behaviour patterns, not similarities, that you had to look for in a murder case—in any case, really. Surely, now he came to think about it, Henry Moleyns had done something different . . . changed his mind about something. . . . He groped about in the back of his own mind, trying to recall an inconsistency on the dead student's part—and then it came to him. The boy had been an enthusiastic supporter of the last sit-in but he wouldn't have anything to do with this one . . . had argued against it in the Library with Hugh Bennett—Roger Hedden and Miss Linaker had both heard him. Vociferous, they'd said. And afterwards, scientist that he was, he'd gone chasing off after the Chaplain and the Modern History man.

"So," said Leeyes, "if he's to be believed . . ."

"Who?" said Sloan absently. An idea had just come to him.

"Ellison," said the Superintendent with the briskness of authority. "If he wasn't after the Hellewell girl, then nobody was and your set-up with Battling Bertha was a waste of time."

"No, it wasn't," replied Sloan, stung into sharp thought in spite of his tiredness. There was something that Crosby had said that must be true—he could see that now. "What it proves, sir, is that Henry Moleyns wasn't in a position to identify who killed him."

Leeyes grunted. "You mean that if Moleyns had known who it was, then whoever killed him would have come after the Hellewell girl in case she had any beans to spill?"

At the back of Sloan's mind was something else.

"The murderer," pronounced the Detective Inspector slowly and carefully, "didn't have to worry about Henry Moleyns being left not quite dead and being able to tell anyone who had attacked him because Moleyns himself didn't know."

"How," began Leeyes, "do you know . . ."

"I was told," said Sloan, light beginning to dawn rapidly now, "only it didn't signify at the time."

"Who by?"

"Stephen Smithers. Reading music."

"That, I suppose," said Leeyes sarcastically, "comes after 'the cat sat on the mat.'"

"He of the sneeze," said Sloan, ignoring this.

"What sneeze?" demanded the Superintendent even more irritably.

"Hay-fever, actually, sir." Sloan had forgotten that Leeyes wouldn't know about the sneeze. "He'd still got it this morning. Very nasty."

"Spare me the medical detail."

"He gets it," Sloan informed him gratuitously, "from wheat."

"I do not care," declared Leeyes with something amounting to passion, "where he gets it from—"

"Canadian wheat, sir. Apparently we've got a lot of it over here now."

"Sloan, neither physical infirmity nor agriculture—"

"Canadian wheat is different from ours."

"The Maple Leaf for ever," snarled Leeyes.

"A new sort of hay-fever, you might say."

"As a hardworking police officer—a very hardworking police officer, Sloan—do I need to know that?"

"No, sir." He, Detective Inspector Sloan, had had time to think, though: time to place what it was that Smithers had told him that he now knew was so important.

"And this Smithers boy, Sloan," continued Leeyes undeterred, "who you say can read music—"

"Not can read, sir," said Sloan, despairing. "Is reading. For a degree."

"And who," carried on Leeyes magnificently, "has hay-fever of Canadian origin . . ."

Sloan gave up the unequal struggle.

"Yes, sir."

Leeyes, who could have given points in tenacity to a working ferret any day of the week, carried on. "He told you who killed Moleyns?"

"No, sir. All he told me was what the murderer's disguise was"—another thought came to Sloan even as he spoke—"and the weapon he used . . . and how he could carry it around without any questions being asked . . . and how it was that

Henry Moleyns didn't recognize him. . . . Crosby thought the same disguise was a ghost."

"And," interrupted Leeyes heavily, "am I going to be privileged to be told as well?"

"For my money, sir, the murderer was dressed in full fencing kit."

"Ahhhhhhhh . . ." A long, slow breath escaped the Superintendent. "That's head-to-foot stuff, isn't it?"

"With mask," said Sloan for good measure. "Just the back of the head shows."

"And the weapon a sword," concluded Leeyes. "An épée or whatever you call them."

"Smithers told me he'd seen a member of the club in the quadrangle, sir, only the penny didn't drop at the time. Come to think of it, so did Bridget Hellewell. Henry Moleyns would think whoever it was, was just giving him a friendly lunge."

"If," said Leeyes neatly, "he's your library man as well, then you might say that sartorially he went from one extreme to the other."

"Miss Linaker," said Sloan, not listening to him, "gave me a clue as well yesterday, only I didn't know what it meant."

"And what," enquired Superintendent Leeyes with ill-feigned patience, "did Miss Linaker say?" The Equal Opportunities Commission might not have made its mark in some quarters, but down at Berebury Police Station Police Superintendent Leeyes was perfectly prepared to believe that Crime as Opportunity included women too.

"It was something out of Shakespeare, sir." Of course the Immortal Bard had had a word for it. Like the Greeks, you couldn't catch him without every human situation, every emotion, covered again and again.

"Not *Hamlet?*" The Superintendent knew his *Hamlet* now as well as he knew the faces of the old lags in Berebury.

"Not *Hamlet*," said Sloan. "*King Henry the Fourth*."

"Don't know it."

"Part One, she said."

"It's always Part One," growled Leeyes. "Well?"

"'Young Harry with his beaver on,'" quoted Sloan, as the door of the room—the absent don's room at Tarsus—opened. A police messenger entered with a sheaf of reports. He was clearly a motorcyclist and was wearing the regulation crash helmet: a latter-day beaver, that's what a crash helmet was. He was dressed in the gauntlet gloves that those of that ilk favour in cold weather and the leggings and boots that somehow went with the job. At the time Sloan saw him for what he was. It was only long afterwards that he realised that he had been looking at a thoroughly modern Mercury—a messenger from the gods.

He had, in fact, only come from Berebury Police Station. Not Olympus.

"From your desk, sir," said the man, handing over the papers. And was gone.

Sloan took them with his free hand in much the same way as a Cabinet Minister opens his dispatch boxes: it was part of the routine that went with the job. Come what may, the routine went on. . . .

With one ear still tuned to the Superintendent, he cast an eye over the top ones. This handful looked pedestrian enough.

The first was from Sergeant Gelven pursuing fraud over at Easterbrook.

The second one was from the constable who acted as Coroner's Officer. Police Constable King had dutifully turned in his report of all that Henry Moleyns had been wearing and had had in his pockets when he was brought into the mortuary.

Detective Inspector Sloan cast his eye down the list of the mundane—until he came to something not quite so mundane.

One receipt for a roll of photographic film left for processing on Tuesday.

At the chemist's shop nearest to the University burgled before midnight.

18
——————

Redoublement

It did all add up.

Lady mathematicians notwithstanding, all that had happened at Tarsus College in the University of Calleshire was adding up. And when he'd done his sums, he, Detective Inspector Sloan, would know the answer—the grand total—and be able to go home to his wife and have a wash and a shave like other men who weren't unlucky enough to be police officers on duty.

A sort of subtotal to the addition sum was provided by Detective Constable Crosby, returning hot-foot from the chemist's shop in Berebury High Street.

"It was the photographers, sir," he announced. "They do their own processing there. The film that Moleyns left there on Tuesday morning has gone."

Sloan didn't feel any more satisfaction than he might have done fitting a piece of a jigsaw puzzle into the hole that was waiting for it. The new piece only added to the picture; it didn't complete it.

"Some bottles of tablets," went on Crosby, "were scattered about, but now they know about the film they reckon that spilling the tablets was just a blind."

"It was the film that the break-in was about," said Sloan with increasing certainty. "Had it been processed?"

Crosby nodded. "Yesterday. I spoke to the boy who did it."

"Well?"

"He thought—he won't swear to it, mind you—that it was just trees."

"Trees?" Sloan couldn't have said off-hand what it was he had been expecting, but it hadn't been trees.

"A wood," said Crosby. "He thinks that they were photographs of a wood."

"Moleyns," declared Sloan with conviction, "had discovered something."

"Yes, sir."

"On his vacation. Abroad."

"Somewhere," said Crosby unhelpfully, "but we don't know where."

Sloan looked at the constable. "We can assume—seeing that someone went to the trouble of stealing his passport—that he went somewhere in Europe that you needed a visa for, and that he didn't want anyone to know where that had been."

Crosby was still unimpressed. "He might only have wanted those photographs for his holiday essay that they all had to do. That was about woods, sir, wasn't it?"

He broke off as he saw Sloan staring at him.

"The essay, Crosby!" breathed the Detective Inspector. "Of course, it was because of the essay. All because of the essay," he said wonderingly. "What clots we've been. Come on—hurry—hurry. . . ."

But Higgins, the porter on the Tarsus gate, was only moderately helpful.

"Professor Mautby brought them in this morning, sir, as usual. The whole pile. It's a bit like school, the way he does that, I always think, but there's no telling Professor Mautby anything."

"No," said Sloan flatly. "The essays . . ."

"Over there." Higgins cocked his head towards a pile of papers. "I just put them on that shelf for them to help themselves. Quite a lot of them have gone already."

"Not Colin Ellison's, I hope," said Sloan urgently. He'd been visited by another idea—one of those misleading pieces of a jigsaw puzzle that looked as if it could fit in anywhere—but was, unbeknown to all, the key piece. Key pieces never looked like key pieces.

"No, sir." Crosby had been thumbing through them. "That's here."

"And the one Henry Moleyns did?" Sloan tried to keep his voice even.

"I know that isn't there," put in Higgins helpfully, "because someone else came down to check on that not five minutes ago. He said it did ought to go back to the poor young gentleman's aunt, so I told him Professor Mautby must still have it. It didn't come back with the others anyway. . . ."

Sloan spun round on his heel. "Where does Professor Mautby live, man? Tell me, quickly."

Time seemed to stand still while the porter ran his finger down the list and gave them the address of a house in north Berebury. It—time—still had the same crystallised quality for Sloan as their police car set off through the streets at a pace that caused bystanders to stare, and to think—quite mistakenly—about the ancient police sport of stolen car chasing.

As they left the centre of the town behind and swung into the approaches of the residential part of Berebury, Sloan said, "Let's have a bit more of our two-tone now, Crosby."

"It'll warn him, sir," objected the constable, "tell him that we're on our way."

"It might save a life if we're late."

Even as the police car was swinging into Acacia Gardens a man was leaving Professor Mautby's house. He was apparently taking courteous farewells of the Professor's wife, clutching something in his hand as he did so. Crosby brought the car to a screeching halt at the Professor's gate and shot out of it towards the man.

It was at that moment that the conventional departure scene disintegrated with the suddenness of breaking glass. Mrs. Mautby stepped backwards, Crosby ran forwards, the man feinted a run away and then turned and hit the constable hard as he advanced. Sloan, bringing up the rear (his son would play in the defence, that was settled), attempted a tackle. It brought the man down all right but it was like trying conclusions with an eel. Crosby, an unhealthy colour now, drew breath and re-entered the fray but in a flash the man was free of Sloan's grip and, ducking back from the constable's approach, he slipped unexpectedly sideways, leapt the low garden wall and was gone.

A bruised but triumphant Crosby flourished a handful of papers. "I got this off him, though, whatever it is."

"That," said Detective Inspector Sloan, "is the essay that Henry Moleyns copied from Colin Ellison's work."

*

In the end it was Professor Mautby who supplied most of the missing pieces of the jigsaw. Sloan had instructed Crosby to drive straight back to Mautby's laboratory at the University while he himself issued staccato orders into the car radio about a man, last seen making off from Acacia Gardens. "Wanted for murder—may be armed—is known to be dangerous—if seen, detain and arrest. Watch his house. . . ."

Professor Simon Mautby was less surprised than Sloan had expected.

"Roger Hedden?" His bushy eyebrows came together. "Yes, Inspector, that fits. I did wonder about him."

"Did you?" said Sloan tartly.

"On my account, not yours."

Sloan waited for enlightenment.

"Someone," said Mautby simply, "was watching me."

"Watching?"

"Call it spying, if you like. Sounds a bit dramatic, I know."

"But that was what it was?" said Sloan, another piece of the jigsaw slotting into place.

"Research has to be done somewhere," said the ecologist obliquely. "I do mine here."

"Yours?" said Sloan.

"Ours," said Mautby firmly.

"That's what I thought," said Sloan. "Hedden . . ."

"Hedden stayed on through the summer vacation when I did." The ecologist grimaced. "Sociologists don't usually work as hard as scientists."

Sloan wasn't interested in academic chestnuts. "A sociologist," he pointed out, "wouldn't know what you were doing."

"True. That's one of the things that made me start to wonder if Hedden was our resident Red."

"What was?"

"Not many sociologists know the botanical name of the humble baked bean."

"And Colin Ellison?" said Sloan, another part of the jigsaw puzzle at hand. "He was watching your work, too, wasn't he?"

"Clever boy," said the scientist reflectively. "Clever enough to spot what I was doing. He was the only one who did, you know. Pity he's a pacifist."

Sloan reserved his judgment on this. He'd had bigger red herrings trawled across his path in his time.

"White mice!" exclaimed Constable Crosby suddenly.

"That was sabotage," said Mautby soberly. "And amateurish, at that. That's when I knew Ellison wasn't the main watcher. If Hedden had been going to destroy my work he'd have waited until I'd finished and stolen it for his people."

"His people?"

"Our future enemies," said Mautby. His eyebrows came together, and he gave Sloan what in anyone less formidable might have been a half-smile. "You don't have anything except friends in peace-time, do you?"

This promising line in university hair-splitting was interrupted by Crosby. "But," he protested, unable to contain himself, "you only do plants."

The Professor turned his way. "Plants equal food, my boy. People need food, especially in war time."

"And your work?" asked Sloan, suddenly both very tired and greatly saddened. If Ellison knew about it, there was every reason why he should.

"On a creeping defoliant. One that wouldn't need spraying from the air as napalm does. All you would have to do is to start it off in enemy territory and it would go on destroying crops on its own. Self-perpetuating—like a plague of locusts, only better."

"What stops it?" Sloan himself would have used the word

"worse" there, not "better," but then, as he reminded himself, he was only a working policeman.

"Ah," said the scientist chillingly, "that still needs some work doing on it."

"And where does Moleyns come in?" said Sloan, still sticking to essentials.

Professor Simon Mautby shook his head. "I don't know."

"His essay . . ."

"A straight crib of Colin Ellison's—for what that's worth. Don't ask me why."

Sloan moved with the bone-weariness of a man who has had no sleep. "May I use your telephone?"

*

"Who did you say?" Superintendent Leeyes sounded disbelieving.

"Hedden," repeated Sloan. "Roger Franklyn Hedden."

"The sociologist?"

"Ah, well, sir . . . that's just it. We think he was a sociologist all right—"

"That's what I—"

"But he was something else as well."

That was when the explosion came. "And you two fumble-fingered fools," bellowed Leeyes, "had him in your precious lily-whites and lost him?"

"You don't take that sort alive," said Sloan confidently. Hedden hadn't even made the mistake of going back to his rooms in Tarsus.

"You can at least try," roared the Superintendent.

"We did try, sir." Crosby was going to have a magnificent bruise tomorrow to prove it.

"And you call yourselves policemen." Leeyes's vocal vigour was undiminished. "What will—"

"Policemen, sir," said Sloan with new assurance. "Nothing more."

"Well?"

"Hedden isn't an ordinary villain."

"Out of your league, were you, then, Sloan?" snapped Leeyes.

"Yes," said Sloan firmly. He'd just realised that that was what made the game—life, if you liked—manageable. It was when you stepped out of your league that you ran into trouble. "We were—and so was young Henry Moleyns."

"And am I going to be told exactly which league this superman Hedden was in?"

"International," said Sloan unhesitatingly.

"I suppose," conceded Leeyes after a moment, "that there's some research going on at all our universities. What is it here?"

"Work," said Sloan, "on a new method of jungle clearance."

"Ah—agricultural purposes."

"Strictly not for the birds anyway," said Sloan ambiguously.

"Mustn't grumble," said Leeyes. "We used something at Walcheren that some Oxford boffin had invented—"

"Same sort of thing," agreed Sloan hastily.

"And what," enquired Leeyes, "had Henry Moleyns got to do with—er—jungle clearance?"

"Nothing at all."

"Sloan," thundered the Superintendent warningly.

"Henry Moleyns," said Sloan, clarifying his own thoughts as he went along, "did his vacation study before he realised he'd stumbled on something sinister."

"What was it?"

"I don't know. Yet. I do know that he hadn't time between getting home on Monday and Thursday morning to do another essay for Professor Mautby, so he nicked all of Colin Ellison's work."

"And copied Ellison's essay on Wednesday night?"

"That's right, sir. And then on Thursday evening he put all of Ellison's things on the fountain parapet."

"On his way to the Chaplain."

"I can only think he was going to consult him about the implications of what he'd found. We know he tried to see the Professor of Modern History, too."

"Bernard Watkinson," said Superintendent Leeyes. "Harpe and his traffic people are always getting on to me about his blood alcohol—he drives like Jehu—but they can never actually catch the blighter at the right moment."

"He was in Military Intelligence in the war, so he'll take a bit of catching," responded Sloan absently. Then he repeated the sentence, as if hearing it for the first time. "He was in Military Intelligence in the war . . . that wasn't a secret."

"Doesn't sound as if it was," said Leeyes caustically.

"I reckon," said Sloan undeterred, "that when Hedden

overheard Henry Moleyns, on top of his row in the Library, try to make appointments with both the Chaplain and a Professor of Modern History who had been in Military Intelligence, he must have wondered what was up with the lad. After all, he was supposed to have been an ecology student."

"It's a different ball-game," said Leeyes, "is nature study."

There were two distinct schools of thought down at Bere-bury Police Station. One was that the Superintendent possessed a sense of humour: the other was that he didn't.

"Er—quite," said Sloan, who wasn't willing to be quoted on this one. "As well as that, sir, Moleyns had already had a noisy argument in Hedden's hearing about not going to the sit-in—and another in the Hall that he may well have heard about."

"Two and two together . . ."

"Make four. A man like Roger Hedden—trained, utterly professional, dedicated—would have followed Moleyns up after that as a matter of course." Sloan coughed. "It is even more likely, sir, that Hedden was acting on instructions from, er, above."

"His master's voice?" said Leeyes.

"They're very thorough."

"I expect the boy was kept an eye on while he was over there," agreed Leeyes tacitly. "They're better at that sort of thing than we are."

"Either that, or Hedden got Moleyns to confide in him instead."

"Then," said Leeyes colourfully, "the beetles would have started to come out of the woodwork all right."

"If," said Sloan, "he persuaded Henry Moleyns to tell him the whole story."

"Sounds to have been too important for the Chaplain, whatever it was," grunted Leeyes, who cut a remarkably fine figure at an official church parade, swagger-stick to the fore, theology nowhere in sight.

"He ought to have gone to Mautby," said Sloan. "He'd have been safe enough with him whatever his secret—I think."

Leeyes grunted again. "It's as well to know your friends as well as your enemies." He himself had sorted out both on the Watch Committee years ago. "By the way, Sloan, I always knew that there was something funny about Roger Hedden."

"A state of nature is a very good disguise," murmured Sloan, "but don't ask me why."

"Not that, Sloan."

"What then, sir?"
"A proper sociologist would have been at the sit-in."

19

Remise

"Third time lucky, sir," announced Constable Crosby, reappearing in Professor Mautby's laboratory, his latest mission completed. "I've got Henry Moleyns' essay notes now. At least, that's what I think they are. They were in Hedden's sitting-room. Well hidden. He'd got a secret cupboard in his drinks cabinet."

The constable laid out on the laboratory bench a rough notebook and some sketch plans.

"Half a hectare of woodland in depth—the complete ecosystem," murmured Professor Mautby, moving over and considering what he saw. "That's what I gave all my second-year students as a vacation study."

The laboratory suddenly seemed a very quiet place as Mautby bent over the papers.

"Yes," said the ecologist at last. "This will be it. There's his preliminary drawing to scale."

Sloan felt as if he had been playing in some particularly vigorous scrummage as he moved stiffly over to the bench and looked at the sketch plan. It meant nothing to him.

On the other hand, it did mean quite a lot to Professor Simon Mautby.

"Henry Moleyns," he began slowly, "chose to study a section of forest, Inspector, or more accurately a clearing in an old forest. In a cold climate."

"East of Cologne," volunteered Sloan.

"And north, I should say. The trees he listed are nearly all coniferous." He pointed to the notebook. "Pines."

"I see."

"I say, this is curious." The Professor peered more closely at Moleyns' notes. "He found that the ground in the forest had once been completely levelled."

"What?"

"And not naturally."

Sloan sat down on one of the bench stools.

"Then," continued the scientist, head still down, "it had been replanted. . . ."

There was a sudden scrabbling sound behind Sloan's back. He spun round with the speed of light—and a rat moved across the front of its cage and back again.

"They don't like visitors," said Mautby.

Sloan exchanged a baleful stare with the rat and then turned back to the bench. "How did Moleyns know that the wood had been replanted?"

"He worked it out. It's not a difficult thing to decide. The trees he examined were all exactly the same age."

"Seedlings, you mean?"

"No."

"Then what?"

"The boy had dug down to several roots." Mautby was totally absorbed now. "The trees he looked at had all been at least two years old when they were replanted."

"A plantation, you mean, then?" said Sloan uneasily.

"Not exactly. That is," continued Mautby with academic detachment, "not according to what Moleyns had written. He records the fact that the trees at the edges of the clearing were somewhat stunted because they had been planted in the shade of older trees."

"But . . ."

"He'd found something else," said Mautby quietly, "when he checked the roots."

The silence in the laboratory was almost palpable now.

Sloan's mind was hundreds of miles away from Berebury and the University of Calleshire. It was in a clearing in a wood that had once been levelled and then replanted with two-year-old trees. "These pines, Professor," he said into the stillness. "About how old are they now?"

The older man looked up. "Between thirty and forty years. All of them."

"And when Moleyns dug down to the roots?"

"I think you can guess, Inspector."

Sloan met his eye and nodded.

"Bodies everywhere he dug." Professor Mautby pushed the dead student's sketch map towards Sloan. "Half a hectare's quite a lot of ground. . . ."

"No wonder he wanted to talk to the Chaplain and Professor Watkinson. I suppose that's why he was in the Modern History part of the Library, too, when Hedden overheard him."

"I think that's what I would want to do, too," said Mautby baldly, "if I were his age and stumbled on a mass grave in a foreign country."

"Hedden's country, do you think?" asked Sloan. The police essentials of the case hadn't left him for a single instant.

"Moleyns very carefully doesn't say where," said Mautby. "So carefully that it must matter. If this is all that he brought back, then I can't tell you any more."

"It isn't." For reasons of his own Constable Crosby had chosen to stand facing the caged rat but he had been listening. "There was something else, sir, wasn't there?"

"Not that I—yes, Crosby, of course there was. I was forgetting." Sloan nodded. Perhaps they would make something of the detective constable, after all.

Constable Crosby produced a plastic bag, duly sealed and labelled, and handed it to Professor Mautby. "The student who never stopped sneezing said it was because of the new Canadian wheat—that was what reminded me."

"We think Henry Moleyns shed a couple of ears of wheat around the place," explained Sloan to the ecologist more diffidently. "Would they tell you anything?"

Professor Simon Mautby adjusted his glasses and closely examined the contents of the package. "*Triticum polonicum*," he said. "No doubt about that."

"Does *polonicum*," asked Sloan cautiously, "mean what I think it means?"

"Polish. The wheat isn't confined to Poland. You get it all round that area."

"I see."

"It doesn't tell us exactly where he'd been or anything like that."

"Just the general direction," said Sloan. "Darkest Europe . . ."

"Even now"—Mautby stared out of the window—"we don't know everything that went on in Europe then. Watkinson will tell you that."

"Moleyns was being very careful."

"Old secrets," said the scientist, "can be as dangerous as new ones."

"Quite." That was handsome coming from him. If Simon

Mautby's creeping defoliant ever got going there would be no food for anyone anywhere.

"Moleyns might have thought some things are best left unknown."

"So must Roger Hedden," said Sloan astringently.

"What—oh, yes, of course." Professor Mautby pointed to the dead student's notes. "Otherwise you realise that Moleyns would have told us where this was, and he doesn't."

"He did try, didn't he?" said Sloan. "But he left it too late."

"Too late?"

"His parting breath," said Sloan, the last piece of the jig-saw slipping into place.

"'Twenty-six minutes'?"

"It means something else besides time, doesn't it?" Sloan said very quietly.

"A line of longitude!" breathed Mautby.

"I saw it on a map today."

"Of course, Inspector. I never thought of that."

"I think 'twenty-six minutes' was the first half of a map reference," said Sloan. He pointed to the notes on the bench. "You do realise, don't you, that we're never going to know the second half?"

*

"The Vice-Chancellor's compliments, gentlemen"—Alfred Palfreyman's parade-ground voice carried effortlessly across the crowded Almstone administration block—"and you're to make your own minds up whether you come out or not."

His assistant, Bert, was busily working away at the locks.

"The doors are open from now on," boomed the Head Porter, "and the police don't want to see any of you at all."

Several hundred pairs of eyes turned his way.

He lowered his stentorian tones a register. "And I'm to tell you that Mr. Hedden has met with a nasty accident."

There was a murmur throughout the ground floor.

"This morning at the railway station. We think he must have dropped his ticket or something."

There was nothing accidental about Palfreyman's use of the royal "we." It was his way of aligning himself, as always, with the angels.

"Just before the express went through." If it was to be put about that the able-bodied Roger Hedden had met his death

)y mischance, then it was not for him, Alfred Palfreyman, to
vonder if the sociologist had fallen or been pushed: but he
:new what he thought.

"He'd gone to catch the local train and forgotten about the
:xpress." You couldn't stop old sergeant-majors thinking but
hey never gave an opinion—not even after Balaclava.

There was another murmur: this time of sympathy.

Palfreyman lowered his voice still further. His next message
vas practically routine. "Would someone pass the word to
'rofessor Teed that there's a television crew outside that wants
o interview him for his opinion on the sit-in."

His last message to those sitting-in in the Almstone adminis-
ration block he suppressed altogether. The sergeant-major in
iim just would not let him relay it to the students. It had been
rom the Vice-Chancellor and had shocked the Head Porter to
he very core.

Palfreyman had been receiving his instructions about what
o say to the undergraduates. The Vice-Chancellor of the
Jniversity of Calleshire had been fresh from hearing the
vhole story of the murders of Henry Moleyns and Peter
Pringle from Detective Inspector C. D. Sloan, Head of the
Criminal Investigation Department at Berebury Police Sta-
ion.

"Tell them, Palfreyman," said the Vice-Chancellor sadly,
'that in the long run obedience to authority is more terrifying
han disobedience."

*

Detective Inspector Sloan, dog-tired now, was consoling a
woman on the loss of a letter. A broken épée had been found,
which was being examined for bloodstains, and now he was
sitting in a pleasant set of rooms in Tarsus College overlooking
the quadrangle where so much had happened.

"I think, Miss Linaker, it is very possible that this letter from
Richard Wordsworth to his brother William that Mr. Pringle's
note mentioned about their other brother—"

"John Wordsworth."

"—who you say was lost at sea."

"Drowned when the East Indiaman *The Earl of Abergaven-
ny* went down," she said.

"Really, miss?"

"Off Portland on February 5, 1805."

"That letter," said Sloan, "about John Wordsworth and Jane Austen . . ."

"Yes?"

"It may never have existed." He was doing this very badly, he knew: out of his depth in the past. "Or at least never been here at Berebury with Algernon Harring's papers." Sloan took a deep breath. "You must appreciate that we have no reason at all, absolutely no reason, to suppose any letter existed. We think it was just a clear piece of opportunism on Hedden's part."

Miss Linaker sighed.

"Moleyns wasn't a wealthy student," said Sloan, "so stealing for gain could have been, er, envisaged and he wouldn't have been around to rebut any suppositions. He knew about the Wordsworth papers, too."

She lifted her head. "He did?"

"The library assistant told him, remember? You and Hedden were both there at the time."

"So we were. I'd forgotten."

Sloan paused, aware that the police view wasn't the only one. "The idea of the letter was important enough to serve for motive. *It* didn't have to exist."

"You've searched for it?" she asked him gruffly.

"Everywhere that we can think of."

"Roger Hedden's rooms?"

"It's not there."

"The Library?"

"Not as far as they can tell." How they could ever tell in libraries was beyond him.

"What about where Henry Moleyns lived?" asked Miss Linaker. "Moleyns comes into it all somewhere."

"It's not there, either." Sloan cleared his throat. "And he doesn't come into the picture in that way, either, miss. We don't think Henry Moleyns had stolen it or anything like that—though I think we were meant to think that. That was the whole idea. And a clever one at that."

"I see."

"Moleyns had—er—other worries, miss." They weren't going to be shared with anyone else at the University—those worries—beyond the Vice-Chancellor, but Sloan did not say this to the Professor of English Literature.

"Colin Ellison," she hurried on. "He seems to have been very active over something."

"Professor Mautby's research," said Sloan dryly. "He's telling his Member of Parliament about it now."

"So Simon's secret is out now, then," said Miss Linaker unexpectedly.

"How did you know that he had one, miss, if I might ask?"

She smiled faintly. "He never kept his laboratory assistants for very long and he let people put it down to his bad temper."

Sloan nodded. Actions always spoke louder than words.

"And he's not really bad-tempered, you know. Only clever."

Sloan let this pass. He'd always felt that the ability to suffer fools gladly was an underrated virtue. It should have been with the cardinal ones . . . perhaps it was, though.

"I suppose," she sighed, "that that puts poor Simon back to square one. Like me."

"Professor Mautby," said Sloan, as bracing as he dared, "does not strike me as a man easily deterred."

She looked up quickly. "Oh, I shall publish, of course. 'Anne's shudderings were to herself, alone.'"

"Beg pardon, miss?"

"That's from *Persuasion*."

"I see."

"But it would have been a very splendid thing to have been able to name that which is nameless and dateless."

"Yes, miss." Whoever Henry Moleyns had found would remain nameless and dateless, too.

And numberless.

An exceeding great army, thought Sloan to himself. (It was his mother who had insisted on his going to Sunday School.) An organised wickedness.

"Inspector . . ."

"Yes, miss?" Out of the window Sloan could see the first of the students beginning to trickle back into Tarsus from the sit-in: the Vice-Chancellor's manifest lack of interest had done the trick there.

"Why did Roger Hedden pretend about the letter and then kill poor Peter Pringle?"

"There had to be a plausible reason for Henry Moleyns' being killed—one that everyone could know about, that is. Hedden wanted everyone to think it was because of the theft of a valuable letter."

"It would have done the trick, too," she said expressionlessly.

"If the Librarian was dead as well," Sloan hurried on—if that sentiment of hers was the tip of an iceberg he didn't want to see the other end—"then, miss, not only did the story about there being a letter hold good but the murder of the Librarian actually lent credence to it." He coughed. "I'm afraid from what I hear that poor Mr. Pringle must have put the idea into Hedden's head himself at High Table."

"Peter? How?"

"When he told everyone about the legal letters with the Wordsworth connection."

"That's right." She nodded vigorously. "Algernon Harring was a lawyer, and so was Richard Wordsworth. At the Staple Inn."

"None of the students could have heard what Pringle said, so it was more likely to be someone from—what do you call it, miss?—the Combination Room."

"John Wordsworth could have been the man she loved," said the Professor of English Literature. "All the evidence—what there is of it—fits. It's just the proof that's missing. . . ."

"It happens to us, too, miss, sometimes, down at the station," said the Detective Inspector with fellow feeling. "What's evidence is one thing, and what's proof—that's different altogether. Sometimes . . ." He paused.

"Yes?"

"Sometimes," he said awkwardly, "you just have to make do with knowing."

*

Superintendent Leeyes was sitting at his desk in Berebury Police Station when Sloan got back from Tarsus College. He looked up at the clock as Sloan walked into the room.

"Your wife's been on the phone, Sloan. If you look sharp about it you've just got time to get her to her relaxation class at the antenatal clinic." He picked up a piece of paper and waved it in front of Sloan. "Would you say that the university sit-in was 'Tumultuous Petitioning'? Because, if so, our legal people say there's an Act of 1661 which says you shouldn't do it. . . ."

ABOUT THE AUTHOR

CATHERINE AIRD had never tried her hand at writing suspense stories before publishing *The Religious Body*—a novel which immediately established her as one of the genre's most talented writers. *A Late Phoenix, The Stately Home Murder, His Burial Too, Some Die Eloquent, Henrietta Who?, A Most Contagious Game,* and *Parting Breath* have subsequently enhanced her reputation. Her ancestry is Scottish, but she now lives in a village in East Kent, near Canterbury.

CATHERINE AIRD

For 15 years, Catherine Aird's mysteries have won praises for their brilliant plotting and style. Established alongside other successful English mystery ladies, she continues to thrill old and new mystery fans alike.

☐	23677	LAST RESPECTS	$2.50
☐	23239	HENRIETTA WHO	$2.50
☐	24083	A MOST CONTAGIOUS GAME	$2.75
☐	24079	PASSING STRANGE	$2.75
☐	24314	A SLIGHT MOURNING	$2.75
☐	23842	HIS BURIAL TOO	$2.50
☐	24316	A LATE PHOENIX	$2.75
☐	23831	THE RELIGIOUS BODY	$2.50
☐	24317	SOME DIE ELOQUENT	$2.75
☐	24078	STATELY HOME MURDER	$2.75

Masters _of_ Mystery

With these new mystery titles, Bantam takes you to the scene of the crime. These masters of mystery follow in the tradition of the Great British and American crime writers. You'll meet all these talented sleuths as they get to the bottom of even the most baffling crimes.

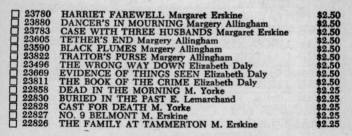

SPECIAL
MONEY SAVING
OFFER

Now you can have an up-to-date listing of Bantam's hundreds of titles plus take advantage of our unique and exciting bonus book offer. A special offer which gives you the opportunity to purchase a Bantam book for only 50¢. Here's how!

By ordering any five books at the regular price per order, you can also choose any other single book listed (up to a $4.95 value) for just 50¢. Some restrictions do apply, but for further details why not send for Bantam's listing of titles today!

Just send us your name and address plus 50¢ to defray the postage and handling costs.